Train Flight

Moon Man

ELIZABETH NEWTON

Order this book online at www.trafford.com
or email orders@trafford.com

Most Trafford titles are also available at major online book retailers.

All scriptures are taken from the Holy Bible.

Printed in the United States of America.

ISBN: 978-1-4269-9708-2 (sc)
ISBN: 978-1-4269-9709-9 (e)

Trafford rev. 03/13/2012

 www.trafford.com

North America & international
toll-free: 1 888 232 4444 (USA & Canada)
phone: 250 383 6864 ◆ fax: 812 355 4082

For J.

Contents

Chapter One

The Invisible Door

To travel through time and space. To journey through history and to other worlds no eye has ever seen before . . . What an adventure. What a freedom. To set your eye on one of those stars way up there in the night sky or just any date you like in a book, set your coordinates and . . .

"Are you sure this is the right road?" Lisa asked from the back seat of the car, contaminating the atmosphere with doubt.

James on the other hand was filled with confidence. And as he was the driver, he was not going to let doubt enter his mind. "Of course I'm sure," he said without taking an eye off the road. "That last turn off was Ardrossan, and now pretty soon, there should be a sign that says Minlaton and that'll be the one we want."

"But it seems like we've been going along this road for too long now, you've gone too far, I reckon."

"Yeah, I remember thinking that last year, but it was right, so . . . just trust me alright." James remained calm. He was a very good driver and he always knew just what he was doing. "And do you mind if I turn the music down for a while, while I concentrate? This road's really dark and the rain's getting heavier."

It was about nine o'clock at night by this time, when James, Lisa and Evelyn were on their way to a shack at Point Turton.

Point Turton is a very small country town by the beach on the other side of the peninsula from Adelaide in Australia. James, Evelyn and Lisa's youth group had travelled there every summer now since 2006—five years ago—for a long weekend to relax and enjoy the sun, the sand and the surf.

After Evelyn, James' younger sister had been interrupted from her book *The Mystery of Space and the Forth Dimension*, she gazed up, deep into the twinkling sky gob smacked by how many more stars you could see out here as opposed to in Adelaide—even with the clouds. She'd seen it before; but every time she did see it, she was in awe and couldn't possibly get her head around it.

She kept this to herself for the time being and said, "I can't believe we're getting so much rain at this time of year."

"I know, it's crazy," said James.

"We definitely need it though," Lisa said from the back, "that's for sure."

"What's the time, James?" asked Evelyn.

He looked at his watch in the light of the car stereo system, "Five past nine."

"Oh far out, we're running so late." Evelyn was annoyed. "By the time we get there it'll be time to go to bed."

"Na, no one will go to bed before midnight," James said.

"Won't there be a 'lights-out' time, since it's a camp though?"

"'Course not, we're young adults, well most of us are young adults now. Summer Camp is always just nothing but relaxation and doing whatever you want."

"What, no . . . *bible study* or anything like that?"

"Not on Summer Camp. That's why I thought you might like to come."

"I've got nothing against the bible studies, it's just . . . well . . ."

"It's alright Evie, you'll like it, trust me. And you've met all the youth before, so it won't be awkward meeting a whole bunch of new people."

"Yeah, I know, it's just that I would have preferred to take along some of my school work to do, I'll get behind."

"But the term hasn't even started for you yet."

"Well . . . some books to read or something . . . about my subjects."

"Evie," said Lisa up back, "When you're on Summer Camp, the rules are 'relax', and 'have fun'. If you do work, there's no point in you being up here at all!"

"That is exactly right," said James.

"Reading relaxes me."

"But surely not school readi—oh, this is the turn off."

James quickly turned the wheel and they found themselves on a very dark road, which eventually turned into a dirt road. Bumpier and bumpier.

It was the beginning of a new year and fourteen year old Evie was in an ultra be-fantastically-organised mode. You know, the ones that get you all excited about a new year and then disappear after the first two weeks.

James, her older brother (who often thought of his sister as a big baby) had worked straight after leaving school, so he seemed to grow up quite quickly and while they were eight years apart, his maturity tripled Evie's. Lisa was nineteen, three years younger than James, and she was going to TAFE, so she understood what Evie was wanting to do.

It was a funny thing—this road they were all now travelling on, seemed to cause a silence in the car. No one talked for some reason. But I bet you can guess that it was because they were all thinking the same thing . . . that this *wasn't* the right road.

James didn't remember a dirt road. Maybe they were in the middle of fixing it up, re-tarring it. Lisa didn't remember there being no street lights. Maybe they just weren't working tonight. Evie thought it strange that they now seemed to be backtracking onto the direction from which they had come. Maybe the road would bend around again at any time.

Three individual thoughts. Three peculiarities. All coincidences? Well they can all easily be explained. But the three young people in the car had doubts.

"You've got us lost," Evie complained.

"No I haven't, that sign said Point Turton."

"Maybe it said *Point Turton* . . . so many *kilometres away*," Lisa suggested.

"I'd notice if it did."

"What was that?" Evie asked, hearing a sound.

"That doesn't sound good," James said doubtfully as the car slowed down to a halt.

James got out and observed a flat tyre. At least the rain was only light now.

"Looking at it won't fix it," Evie said leaning out the window.

"I'll need some help getting some luggage out of the boot so I can get the spare out."

Evie moaned as she slumped out of the passenger seat—all rugged up in beanie, scarf and woolly jumper. She looked just like a walking pile of clothes.

"What did you do with the keys?" James asked. He had given Evie his second set of keys to look after—the set that had the boot key on it.

Evie reached her hand inside her pocket. Out came a used tissue, a little purse with her pocket money in, a plastic whistle, and then the keys.

"What have you brought *that* for?" James asked grabbing the whistle. "Didn't I steal that from you and secretly put it in the bin?"

"I found it. In the bin, you big thief. I thought I'd use it to . . . um . . . use it in case of an emergency."

"Right," he said, not convinced. He was suspicious that she was going to use it to wake him up early in the mornings. He was the sleeper-innerer—she was the early-riser. She could drive him crazy with that stupid whistle. "I think I'll keep it here in *my* pocket," he said.

"No, it's mine. That's not fair." Evie wanted to use it to wake him up early in the mornings, but she wasn't going to tell *him* that.

"Come on, you two," Lisa called. "Stop arguing." She started to unpack the boot, while Evie walked a little way back along the road to see what it was that they had run over.

She let her eyes adjust to the dark moonlit road, but even then it was really hard to see. She saw the outline of a large . . . thing—difficult to make out. Larger than the normal stones you'd find on a dirt road, so she assumed it must have been the culprit. She knelt down, and picked it up. It was warm. She threw it down with a gasp.

"Don't wander off, Evie," James called.

"I'm just looking, to see what it was." She looked up and further ahead. There were a couple more of them, scattered. She supposed they were rocks—well, what else could they be? But they almost looked like lumps of coal.

James and Lisa were making a lot of noise, Evie thought. Unpacking and packing, pumping and riveting, clattering and clanging.

But it took her just a few small moments to realise that not all the sounds she heard were coming from the direction of the car. There was something else. Straight ahead of her. In fact, the large, warm rock things formed a sort of scattery trail closer toward the sounds. She looked behind her at James kneeling at the front end of his car; Lisa, handing him the required tools; and then straight ahead again, where the strange sounds became more and more enticing. There was nothing but landscape in front of her, nothing but dry open fields and nature all around. But the sounds were that of machinery, and as she slowly walked further along the road past the guiding rocks, the sound grew stronger and she found herself walking to the slow and even pace of the rhythmic rattling hum of an engine of some sort.

*Choofety **chuff** choofety chuff*
*Choofety **chuff** choofety bang!*
*Choofety **chuff** choofety chuff*
*Choofety **chuff** choofety bang!*

The sound was so near, *yet it must be miles away* because she couldn't see anything for miles. Land and sky to her left. Land and sky to her right. Land and sky is all she could see—nearly all in blackness. Lisa and James were getting smaller and smaller as she walked further and further towards the sound. That easy hum—not loud, just stronger with every step . . .

c**huff** choofety chuff
Choofety **chuff** choofety bang!

She bent over and picked up one of the warm rocks and held onto it. With another gasp of fright, she noticed it glow a little and fade. Glow . . . and fade. Glow . . . and fade. It grew hotter and hotter in her hand and eventually it was so hot that she could feel her skin burning and she had to toss it away. She looked down at her hand and nursed it, while out the corner of her eye, she saw a flash of light and heard a sound along with it. If you've ever heard a tennis ball hitting a tin roof—it sounded just like that.

She looked up. Nothing.

She picked up another one of those glowing rocks—warmer now in her hand, and she threw it, and this time, she saw the small flash of light as the rock hit . . . mid-air . . . ?

She frowned, bent over to pick up another rock to test it again but . . .

"Do you mind not doing that?" a voice said. A male voice. English accent.

She looked all around her. There was no one. She glanced back to the car over behind her. It was not much more than a speck now. But no one was in sight . . . until she turned back around to the way she was facing before, and standing a little way in front of her was a man wearing driving-goggles. Standing out in the middle of nowhere, like herself.

"D-doing what?" she asked sheepishly.

"Throwing that debris at my craft."

Evie looked around again, confused and slightly nervous. "What craft?"

"My beautiful Blackerby, my . . . oh . . . sorry. Never mind."

Evie felt afraid. She frowned, and narrowed her eyes and said, "I think I should be getting back. Goodbye." She turned on her heels and pretended she hadn't seen anyone, shoulders hunched with the cold, and hands in her pockets.

The man called after her. "You must think I'm pretty loopy, mustn't you?"

She stopped, turned her upper body back. "Where on earth did you come from?" *Curiosity killed the cat*, she thought to herself uneasily.

"Oh, well that's a long story. Are you out here all by yourself?"

"No. My brother and friend are over there. We broke down. Well, not really, it was a flat tyre."

"That happened to me. Not the flat tyre, the broken down bit."

Evie looked at him like he was some kind of nut. "Your . . . craft you mean?"

"You think I'm some sort of nut don't you."

". . . No."

"Yes you do." He shrugged, "I would if I were you."

". . . Okay."

"Come here and I'll show you that I'm not."

Evie backed away and shook her head timidly. "No way."

The man didn't have anything to say for a few seconds. He looked disappointed—surprised as well. He changed the subject.

"By your accent I'd say you were from . . . Australia?"

". . . Yeah, this is Australia."

"This is Australia?"

". . . Yes."

"Where in Australia?"

"Not one hundred percent sure, but hopefully near Point Turton."

"Why hopefully?"

"Well because . . . I'd better be getting back to my brother and Lisa . . . where are you trying to get to?"

"Serothia."

"Never heard of it. Is it near here?"

"Well I wouldn't know would I?"

"Oh I . . . suppose not. Is it somewhere round the York Peninsula?"

"I don't think so, is that anywhere near the Coma Berenices constellation?" He was smiling slightly now, as if he was playing with her.

"The *what*?

"Well clearly, you haven't heard of it, so I've fallen short."

Evie was busting to find out what all this was about, but she kept it concealed and merely shook her head as if she was dreaming. "I'd better get back."

"It was your own curiosity that made you wander out this far wasn't it?"

The stranger was making Evie feel more and more uneasy. She knew never to talk to strangers, but for some reason she felt she couldn't just run away. He must have been a madman. He looked in his early thirties and could definitely do her harm if she got closer. But he showed no signs of wanting to cause her harm. He may need help, she thought. Maybe he's broken down a mile or so away and doesn't know how to ask for help. Maybe he needs mental help. He did look kind of harmless . . . in a funny sort of way. But all the same . . .

"I've got to get back to the car, my brother will be worried."

He glanced over her shoulder, squinting his eye a little. "Right, that would be the car that was just over there a moment ago?"

Evie whipped her head around wide eyed and she panicked. The car that she had come in, along with Lisa and her brother—the small distant figures that they were, had gone.

She turned her whole body now and took a few steps toward the road. "No . . . what's going on, where are they. Why would they leave without me?" Her breathing quickened and her heart was pounding. She turned again to face the stranger, and to her horror, he was now nowhere to be seen.

She gasped. She thought she'd imagined him. But she was certainly not imagining that she was alone. She ran back up to the road and looked for the car. "They wouldn't leave me here," she said to herself breathlessly, "James!!" she called. "Jaaaaaaaammes!!!"

Her voice became weak like she was about to cry in worry. "What's going on, where are they?" She ran back to where the stranger had stood, and then turned back towards the road. "Hello? Is anyone there? HELLO!!? Oh my goodness, what do I do? HELLO!!!?? JAA . . ."

"My my, you *do* have a loud voice," a voice said from behind her. She turned and the stranger was back, but now she thought she *must* be dreaming. His upper-body was on a slant and his lower-body was completely . . . not there. As if he was leaning out of a window and everything but his head and chest was nonexistent. Then suddenly he made a little jump and the rest of him appeared, but now he was leaning against . . .

"How did you do that?"

"Do what?" he said worriedly.

"Well, you just . . . came out of thin air."

He looked relieved, "Oh . . . not out of thin air. What's all the fuss about?"

"What do you think? James and Lisa have just *gone*. I'm all alone and I don't know what to do."

"They didn't leave without you. Well, not deliberately."

"Well then what else happened? Are they invisible like you?"

"Do you really want to know."

"You've done it haven't you . . . you've done something. Give them back!" she demanded. She huffed and then said quietly, "Yes, I really want to know."

"Sure?"

"Of course I'm sure."

"Your brother and your friend are most probably trapped in a chronic continuous repulisaricular time spiral."

All was silent but the pattering gallop of a rabbit darting across the road.

". . . What"

"A chronic continuous repul-oh, never mind. But don't worry, I'm going to find them."

"You're going to help me find them?" she said, no where near convinced of this man's sanity.

"Oh, I'm going to find *everyone*. Just as soon as I've completed my repairs."

The man disappeared again. And this time, it was right in front of Evie's own eyes. She gasped, eyes and mouth open wide. She hesitated forward. *I must be dreaming* she thought, *it's the only explanation*. One step, after another step, she drew closer to . . . nothing—where the stranger had disappeared. There was nothing there. Until Evie took one more step and out the corner of her eye, she saw light. When she turned her head to the left, it was the strangest thing. There was a vertical and very narrow shaft of yellowy light. It seemed to be hovering in mid-air and at the top and bottom, the light cornered at a right angle so it looked like the outline of a rectangle—one side missing. She was about to raise her hand up to see if she could touch it, but suddenly, the sliver of light became a larger opening of light as the stranger burst through and Evie staggered back as something hit her. It was a door.

"Ooh, I'm sorry did I hurt you?"

"Yes."

"Well you *would* stand right behind the door!"

"The door?"

"I was just about to say all fixed and ready to go, are you coming?"

"Coming where?"

"Wherever I need to go to find your friend and your brother."

Evie looked scared and unsure of herself. Everything was telling her not to trust this man. After all, he was a stranger and it would go against everything she had ever been taught about strangers.

She shook her head, "I can't go with you."

The stranger leaned a little further out of the door and said softly and reassuringly, "I realise your dilemma. However, I don't know if you've noticed this but . . . you don't have anywhere else to go."

Chapter Two

A Billion Diamonds In The Sky

There was one step up and suddenly, Evie was in a narrow room with old fashioned décor. There were cosy looking lounge chairs lining the two longer walls, a standard lamp, a floor to ceiling bookshelf and a round rug in the middle with detailed pattens all over it. There were six little square windows along the walls above the lounge chairs. If you can imagine how much three and two metres are, the room looked about three metres long and two metres wide. In short, it was absolutely charming.

The stranger had taken her hand to help her up the small step and now squeezed past her and said, "This way." He walked past the lounge chairs and the bookshelf, opened another door at the other end of the room and disappeared.

Evie hesitantly followed. Although she felt relaxed by the cosy atmosphere, she couldn't get it out of her mind that this was a terrible trap that she was walking into of her own free will.

Now at the door, which had wafted closed behind the stranger, Evie clutched the heavy old metal handle. She pushed on the door gently and as she did so, that sound again came flooding out:

*Choofety **chuff** choofety chuff*
*Choofety **chuff** choofety bang!*

She opened the door slowly and the sound was louder than ever. In front of her was a big round mushroom-shaped structure with controls and buttons and little lights all over it mounted on a solid metal cylinder. This was what was responsible for all the noise. In the centre, rising out of it was a thick steel pipe painted black, that looked like a flew of a fire place or woodstove, which reached right up to the ceiling. The pipe was between Evie and the stranger. He was fiddling with some controls on another control panel section which was against the far wall straight ahead and on that wall was a wide window that stretched from corner to corner. Out of it, she could see the night sky and the dark country fields—the landscape by which she was surrounded just moments ago. The room was even smaller than the first room but somehow it seemed quite spacious—or spacious enough to move around easily—the man she was with certainly wasn't acting like he was cramped. The floor was metal and the walls were made of wood panelling. It looked old fashioned, yet filled with advanced electronic equipment.

Evie was too astounded to speak or even ask, *where am I and what is all this?*

The stranger continued to press buttons and pull levers and he was mumbling some words under his breath. There was a *ding!* and suddenly a long thin strip of paper came shooting out of a slot on the control panel, and the stranger took it in his hand and examined it.

"A-ha!" he exploded and hopped around to face the thing in the middle of the room. He started moving his index finger over a long horizontal pad, kind of like the sensor pad on a laptop that controls the curser on the screen. Then he tapped a few buttons and said, "You ready?"

Her brow creased up significantly, showing worry, "R . . . r ready for what?"

"To go."

She frowned, "I suppose I'm ready, if you are."

The stranger's eyebrows turned down at the ends, "Well I'd feel more confident if you'd have just said yes."

"Okay then, yes."

Evie could not imagine what she was heading into. She was with a complete stranger, in an unknown vehicle which was apparently formless, she had had no explanations, no idea of who or what this man was, and he was asking her if she was *ready?*

Suddenly, there was a jolt, followed by a few bumps and then a groan, which sounded a bit like a proud sea lion. And then the wide window tinted so it could no longer be seen out of while the *chuff choofety chuff choofety chuff choofety bang!* pulsed steadily in the background. Evie could see the stranger smiling just behind the steel pipe in the middle of the room.

"Thank you Lord," he said softly, then a little louder, "Thank you *Lord,* it's working!"

"It *is?*" Evie said, because the engine—if it was an engine, sounded pretty sick and worn out to her; but her voice wasn't heard.

Suddenly, all the bumps and the unsettling noises ceased, leaving the very gentle rhythm of *chuff choofety chuff choofety chuff choofety bang!* chugging softly and calmly in the background.

Evie's eyes finished up on the stranger's and he looked back at her. When their eyes met, Evie's stomach jumped. She was frightened, bewildered, uncertain and suspicious. On top of all this, she was worried for James and Lisa as well. It was very quiet in there now and she didn't have to speak up much. She used her quiet little kitten voice out of all her confusion, "Are . . . are we moving?"

"Yes, we're moving."

"Sounds like we've *stopped*."

"Oh no, all that noise was just us taking off."

"Oh . . ." she stared down at the floor. Then she looked up at him again and barked, "Taking *OFF*?"

"Yes," he smiled. "I suppose it's about time I owed you an explanation." He walked around the centre machine with his hands behind his back.

"Is this some kind of hover-craft?" she guessed.

"Nnnnnno, not exactly . . ."

"A jet plane thingy?"

He shook his head.

"But how can it be *anything*, there was nothing there, in the field, I didn't see anything."

"Well if you gave me a chance to talk, I could tell you," he said with a smirk as if Evie amused him.

She was quiet. And ready.

"Technically, you're in a space ship, but I like to call it my Train, which is more exciting than you think," he said, quick to defend himself. "On a planet called Minazga, the word *train* doesn't refer to a large form of transport that runs along tracks. The word means *wonder* and in a more ancient dialect, it means *revealing the wonder and glory of God*.

". . . A spaceship?" Evie said sceptically and as if her mind had only caught up to this much.

"Yes. But it also travels in time."

". . . a Train?"

"Good name, don't you think?"

". . . A planet called Minazga?"

"Quiet little planet. Very humble people."

". . . Time!?"

The stranger staggered back. "Alright, alright, no need to shout."

"I must be dreaming."

"Now, if I got a dollar every time someone said that . . ."

"Is it? Is this a dream?"

The stranger busied himself at the centre console. "No. I'm sorry, if you were hoping for one."

"Are . . . are you an alien?"

"Well that depends on what *you* are."

"I'm not an alien."

"No I don't mean that. I mean what planet are you from. I would say Earth as a guess, seeing as that's where we were when I met you."

"You mean we're not there anymore?"

"Well we've left the atmosphere, if that's what you mean."

"What?!" Evie ran to where the windows were, but as they were tinted now, she looked at the stranger with a questioning expression.

He shrugged, smiled and pushed a button, which had happened to be just under her little finger.

Slowly, the thick glass of the window began to change tone. It lightened from black and blank to a normal see-through window revealing the black night outside. But it wasn't just the black night. There were a lot more stars than usual. There had to be thousands of them in sight. Billions even. A billion diamonds in the sky.

Evie was speechless, but eventually she breathed out in total disbelief, "We're floating in space."

"Not floating," the stranger said, "orbiting. We're orbiting the Earth. If you go and look out the side window from the other room, you'll see the Earth itself."

Evie looked up wide-eyed at her captor and then bolted for the door from which she had entered. She was back in the first room, and as she hopped onto one of the lounge chairs on her knees and gazed out the window there, she saw the most awesome and breathtaking sight.

The Earth. So big in front of her, yet so far away. She could see the shape of Australia—the way it looks in Geography text books and Atlases, but with one additional incredible and alarming feature . . . it was *real*.

Evie could not take her eyes away. She didn't even want to blink, the view was so spectacular. There were clouds sweeping slowly across the top of South Australia and she could see many colours covering the surface of the land. But what astonished her the most, was the perspective it gave her. Seeing South Australia and the approximate position of her little Adelaide hometown compared with the rest of the land and all the water—her home on the giant ball suspended in the shadow of the sun.

She felt the stranger standing behind her now and she repeated something she had heard him say earlier. "Revealing the power and glory of God." There was a silent moment before she spoke again, "It *is* a good name."

Chapter Three

The Decision

In that moment, Evie had forgotten everything. She'd forgotten about James and Lisa being trapped in . . . whatever it was they were supposed to be trapped in; she'd forgotten about the Summer Camp and Point Turton; and she'd forgotten that the man she was with—in whose hands her life was now in suddenly, was a complete stranger.

"Out the other window look," the man said, "you can see the moon."

Evie hopped off her couch and onto the other one opposite. It was a full moon and very bright, and it seemed just that little bit bigger and closer than how she'd seen it before. It was like a whole new realm of thinking. On Earth, the view of the moon and outer space was all she'd known for fourteen years. But out here, it was like seeing it all for the first time. The moon was the same friendly moon with the same friendly but gloomy face on it, but it looked different. How was it just hanging there, suspended in space, reflecting the sun's light in all its shining brilliance? It looked more powerful, more substantial, more like a planet than just a moon. It deserved a name like a planet—being so beautiful and all. But then it crossed Evie's mind that calling it simply *the moon* gave it its deserved esteem. It set it apart from all the other moons in space that she knew of.

An "I can't believe this" slid out of Evie's mouth.

"You haven't seen *anything*," the man said, with that smirk again. "You ought to see Tragon's moon. They call it the golden ball, its surface looks yellow but it's actually just an illusion. There used to be stories that it was the only moon actually made of cheese, but it's not true of course."

Evie smiled.

"Argneras is the only moon made of cheese."

Her smile dropped.

Then, with another subtle shake of her head in disbelief, she asked reluctantly, "Is . . . is Tragon where you're from?"

"Tragon?" he laughed. "No. You know I'm less of an alien than you might think. I come from a place not so far off from where you're from. It's closer than you think."

". . . You're a moon-man," she guessed. But then she realised how dumb it sounded.

The stranger just laughed, didn't reveal anything more. "I have to take her down now, if you're done looking?"

"Down where?"

"Back to Earth—once I've got the time right."

Evie frowned and gently shook her head, "Whatever . . . whatever you have to do."

The man turned on his heals and headed back into what you could call the engine room, (since it was where the engine seemed to be), but then he turned back to his passenger and asked, "What's your name by the way?"

Evie had returned her focus to the view of the Earth out the window and absent-mindedly said over her shoulder without taking her eyes off her magnificent home, "Evie Bamford."

"Evie," the stranger repeated. "Short for Evelyn I presume. Nice enough name, I suppose."

She had taken no notice of what he had said and she didn't realise that a golden opportunity to ask him what *his* name was had just passed her by. He disappeared into the engine room leaving Evie still in awe of the sight.

The stranger pressed a couple of buttons, wrote down a few notes and then pulled a lever and suddenly there was a thrust of the mechanics and the ship swooped down towards South Australia again.

The ride was smooth as. All Evie noticed was the planet appearing to become closer and she began to see more detailed marks on the land. All of a sudden, there was a tiny jolt and Evie guessed that they had just passed through to Earth's atmosphere. But it surprised Evie beyond description to realise, that now they were in the sky, it was day time. The windows began to automatically tint again and after a few feeble attempts to try and un-tint them, she ran into the engine room where the stranger still was.

"We must have been up in the sky longer than I thought, it's the next day already!" she said in alarm.

"Correction," said the stranger calmly, manipulating some controls, "it is the same day."

"What do you mean?"

"I mean, it's the same day." He swung his arm down with style on a lever which made the craft jolt again. "Shall we go?"

Evie's face surrendered into a 'whatever' expression and she followed the stranger right through the first room, down the little step and out the door. He slid a pair of trendy looking glasses on, turned back to the Train and Evie heard the door being closed. For some reason, she didn't look back straight away at the craft she had just emerged from. Perhaps it was a moment she wanted to build up to. She could feel a tingling feeling between her shoulder blades, the stranger returned to her side and after a few seconds, she turned around to see . . .

Nothing. Nothing but country side. The sun's late afternoon rays beaming off the fields of green grass and bright yellow canola.

"What's going on here?" Evie said. "This is like last night, you disappeared into thin air and now we've just appeared from thin air, haven't we? What is this, an invisible spaceship?"

"Not . . . invisible, it's more like . . ." The stranger looked at his watch. "Shooting star, we've got to get moving." He headed off as if he knew exactly where he was and where to go next.

Evie on the other hand, felt like she was in the middle of nowhere—where they left off, was the only information she could fathom. She hurried along to catch up with him, and got very hot very quickly. She still had layers and layers of clothing on from the night before . . . or whatever night it was, and she had to start shedding them or she'd bake in the afternoon sun. "You haven't explained your spaceship to me. You haven't explained what we're doing or where we're going. In fact, you haven't even explained to me *who you are!*"

"You're quite right there, I haven't."

"Well?"

"It's a difficult question for me to answer." He kept on walking, taking wide purposeful strides that Evie had trouble keeping up with.

"Well try. I have to know if I'm going to trust you."

"Well I'm no one real special. I'm quite clever, I eat my veggies, I love walks, I'm a huge fan of The Beatles, and I can't stand those ridiculous toy computer things that you're supposed to feed every hour or they die."

"I don't mean that."

"Well what do you mean?"

"You could start with your name."

He stopped, looked back at her, and answered in a matter-of-fact tone, "I'm the Captain."

"The Captain. *The Captain of the Train.*"

"That's right." He started walking again.

"Yeah but . . . Captain what? What's your name, what do I call you?"

He stopped and turned again, this time making Evie almost bump into him. Suddenly he was stern. "You will call me Captain because I am the Captain of my ship. It's the correct form of address." And with that he continued walking again, with a spring in his step.

"But you don't have a crew."

"That's not the point."

Evie realised shortly that they were now by the side of the country road that James was driving on when they had realised they might be going in the wrong direction. She could guess by a familiar array of dry bushes not far from the road's edge. However, she doubted that suddenly, when she remembered all the strange glowing bits of rubble.

"All that stuff's been cleaned up," she said with a puzzled look on her face.

"What stuff?"

"That weird stuff I saw last night along the road, which led me away from James and closer to you. It was the strangest thing, when I picked it up, it got warm in my hand *and* they started glowing."

"Oh," the Captain said gravely, "so *that's* where I lost the fuel."

Evie's neck protruded a little. "Fuel?"

"From the Train. It would have been Carnane fuel from when I went out of control and crashed."

"Well someone's been collecting it up, it's not here now."

The Captain sighed.

". . . That is . . . if we *are* in the same spot."

"Yes, we're in the same spot but didn't you hear me before? You and your brother haven't been past here yet. The Train hasn't even crash landed, so how *could* the coal be here?"

Evie frowned intensely. Then slowly, the creases in her brow began to iron out and she lifted her head up sluggishly to look at the Captain, wide-eyed. "The same day," she whispered in amazement.

"She gets it!" he said throwing his hands up.

"Well there's no need to be so mean about it."

"You're right, I'm sorry. It's just that I've had . . . no, I'm not going to say that because everyone says that don't they?"

"Say what?"

The Captain put on a dumb dreary voice. "I've had a bad week, I've had a bad day. My wife's just left me or my play-station blew up."

"Is that what you were going to say?"

"No, I was going to say my ship crash landed." He suddenly smiled, "but you're right, that's no excuse to be mean." He turned, put his hands inside his pockets and started examining the ground.

After a few moments of silence, Evie politely asked, "So when you said . . . time . . . you meant . . ."

"Yes, the Train can travel through time," he replied while busily carrying on.

"And so . . . tonight . . . later on . . . James, Lisa and I will be heading along this road . . . until we stop and get out . . . and I wander along here and . . ."

"Precisely. Only we won't be hanging around that long."

"Aw, why not? That'd be *so* cool!"

"It's far too dangerous." He started jumping up and down in different places, as if testing the stability of the ground.

Evie had gotten the feeling that the Captain wasn't listening to her, being so absorbed and focussed on what he was doing. But nevertheless, he answered her questions and kept up the conversation, just without disturbing himself by looking up at her. She dawdled around rubbing her soles over a few stubby bits of dry bush.

"Where are you from?" she asked out of the blue. "I don't believe you're a moon man." She observed him making funny, random gestures into the air, jumping up and down again and then sometimes dropping down onto his hands and knees all of a sudden and putting his ear to the ground. "Although I have to admit, you act like one . . . but then again, I don't know what moon men act like. All the same, no living thing could survive on the moon. And even if they could, the same creature couldn't survive in *this* atmosphere. You said *closer than I think* . . . I wonder what that means. You look human enough, that's for sure."

Evie, still observing the Captain's inspections put her hands on her hips, cocked her head to one side and finally asked, "What are you doing?"

"I'm trying to figure out where the Seroth gate is and how it is being driven and what's driving it."

Evie's eyes wandered. She wished she hadn't asked.

"Can you remember exactly where you were along the road when your brother stopped the car?" the Captain then asked.

Evie jogged over to him and looked around on the ground next to the road. "Er . . . I think about . . . here. But it looks so different in the day time, I can't be abso*lutely* sure."

The Captain pulled some sort of contraption out of his coat pocket. It was about the size of a T.V. remote control and had a yellow and a red light on the top and various buttons underneath.

Evie watched as he walked slowly along the road side staring at the gadget. Now and again it would beep a couple of times. He looked so determined, as if he was searching for a lost ring in the dirt that was worth more than any amount of money in the whole world.

Just when Evie thought he was looking unsure of himself, the gadget beeped rapidly and he stopped in his tracks. He knelt down on the ground and scanned the gadget over the little area and suddenly with great exclamation that made Evie jump, he said, "Ah ha!" and he jumped up and headed straight back to the Train.

"What now?" said Evie following after him.

He did not answer. She merely saw him disappear onto the Train. She wondered what it was he'd found and glanced back at the road. Suddenly, she had a moment to herself, and she used it to try and comprehend everything that had happened in the last thirty minutes of her life. Then she shook her head in wonder and disbelief and muttered to herself, "The same day." She wished she could hang around until late that night to see James' car come down the wet road in the dark. Then she could hide and even find out what it was that flattened the tyre. She particularly wanted to hang around so that she could be certain in her mind that all this *was* in fact real. Captain 'who-ever-he-was' just *said* that it was the same day, but so far she'd seen nothing that actually proved it.

She turned around to head for the Train, and then she freaked. Nothing was there. That is, she *couldn't see* where the Train was.

"Captain?" she called.

No reply.

She walked a little way closer and then soon raised her arms out in front of her as if she was walking in the dark. *The Captain didn't have to do this, how did he know where the Train was?* She felt ridiculous. There she was, out in the middle of nowhere, wandering around looking for an invisible spaceship. If someone was to pass by, they might have thought some of her friends had blindfolded her for a party game and then ran away for some cruel unfunny joke.

Suddenly, her fingertips hit something, they crumpled up and hurt for a while. She spread her fingers out and felt the surface with her hands. It was metal and it felt smooth and flat. She followed the surface along to her right until she came to the end and then she felt her way around to the opening. Next, she could see the inside of the Train. She jumped up into it and found the Captain in the engine room, with a large piece of paper unfolded and laid out on the floor.

"What are you doing?"

"That was the last link in the chain. The last piece of the puzzle," he said.

"What was?"

"Your brother and his friend."

"It's Lisa."

"Alright *Lisa* and his friend. What's important is that I've found it!"

"Found *what*?"

"What? Oh! Well it's a map see?"

Evie joined him on the floor.

"This planet has been converged by various electronic impulses from an alien source. It would explain the strange on-and-off changes in the weather that you may have been noticing. I've pinpointed every spot where someone has disappeared in the last few weeks. I just needed one more spot to get a strong enough signal. Now I know exactly where they've been taken to . . . well, the rough vicinity."

"You mean there've been others?"

"Other than Lisa and Jamie? Yes, dozens. And there's likely to be dozens more, maybe hundreds if I don't hurry up and make a move."

"Where to?"

"Serothia, Evelyn, do try and keep up. Just got to set the coordinates and I'll be off."

"*You'll* be off? Me as well you mean."

"Ah no, Evelyn, you'd be much safer if you stayed here."

"Stay here while you go to Serothia?!" she exclaimed, and then quietened. "Where's Serothia?"

"No time. Evelyn, you'd better get off the Train now and wait for me."

The Captain had returned to the centre controls and the Train was beginning to roar again.

"Wait for you, are you kidding? I've got to find James and Lisa!"

"Evelyn, I can manage on my own. You'll be safer here. Just don't interfere with yourself if I don't get back before your car comes along. And that's not a suggestion, that's an order."

"But I want to stay with you. I don't want to be left out here all on my own!"

The Captain walked a little distance, stood right in front of Evie and put his hands on her shoulders. "Trust me Evelyn, this is for your own good. I don't know how dangerous this is going to be."

Evie fell quiet. She looked up into his eyes and saw how serious he was. She was frustrated and worried and confused and frightened. She'd never been faced with danger before—not *real* danger. The most dangerous thing she'd done was write notes to her friend in class. Then she reflected deeper. She'd actually cheated in her last maths test. That was the most dangerous thing she'd ever done. And she regretted it.

She swallowed it down, swept it under the rug and tried to forget about it. "So what do I do," she said, "just stand out there and wait for James and Lisa to return?"

"No, you wait for *me* to return. You can't stay here, this isn't your time."

"Oh yeah," she realised. She hung her head and started walking slowly towards the door.

The Captain returned to the central console and flicked buttons and pulled levers—preparing to take off again. He'd thought Evie had left, yet suddenly, she came running back in with a strong and determined voice. "You can't show me the Earth from space and fly right past the moon, entice me into this magical machine and invite me to come with you, and *then* ask me to stay behind!"

He frowned, "Did I entice you?"

She nodded.

Then the Captain sighed apologetically, "I'm always doing that." Then he looked straight into her still-determined eyes. He raised one eyebrow and said with the slightest, slightest smirk, "Are you sure?"

Again, she nodded.

"Hold on tight then."

There was a thud from the direction of the Train's opening—the door shutting; and then the roaring of the engine and the floor beneath them shook and so for the first time, Evie did just what she was told. She held on tight.

Chapter Four

Tea Party In Space

"You might want to look out the window now," said the Captain, after a few minutes, still hopping from one control to the next.

Evie, terrified out of her wits said with a stutter, "I . . . I c can't, the windows are black."

"Try that switch right . . . there."

She looked to where he was pointing. Then she looked up at him, and then back down to the control. Then she smiled within herself and went for the switch.

The windows changed from black to see-through, and it's difficult to describe what Evie saw, because there was nothing around that she recognised as home—her home solar system that is. She was speechless when she laid eyes upon the most beautiful nebula she'd ever seen. Or perhaps it was only the most beautiful nebula she'd ever seen because it was the only one she'd actually seen in real life. It could have been the most boring nebula (if there's such a thing) if it were just a picture. But this wasn't a picture of a nebula in a text book or on the internet; this was a nebula that was right in front of her eyes, wafting out there in space.

The Captain turned a sort of steering wheel on the front control panel and the Train slowly wafted to the right and now in full view of the window, there was a big bright orange planet. Evie's jaw dropped without her even realising.

"Where are we?" she said.

"We're now in Sector B-172239, the northern constellation Coma Berenices, in a galaxy called M64. In other words Evelyn . . . you're a long way from home."

"How far?" she practically whispered.

"From Earth? Seventeen million light-years."

"M64. Sounds like a road."

"It's called the Black Eye Galaxy by the astronomers on Earth."

"And is that Serothia?"

"Yes. Sixth planet from its sun. Very dull, very humid. But something's wrong down there and we need to find out what it is."

"Are James and Lisa down there?"

"Possibly. The question is, how do we find them?" Then he muttered in a lower voice, it wasn't necessary for Evie to hear, "Please help me out with this one, I can't waste time searching the entire face of the planet."

Just then, there was a beeping from the front control panel. The Captain attended to it straight away. When he comprehended what had caused the beeping, he smiled and then raised his eyebrows as if in pleasant surprise. "Thank you," he said.

"What does that mean?" Evie asked referring to the beeping.

"It's the radio scanner, and there's an object on there see? Much bigger than the Train."

"What is it? Is it dangerous?"

"I tuned the scanner to the readings of this," he held up the gadget he had been using back on Earth. "So that means, it's not the planet we want, it's *that*." He pointed to the little dot on the radio scanner."

"Yes, but . . . what . . . *is* it?"

"Judging by its size and apparent position I'd say it was a satellite."

"So what are you going to do?"

"We need to get the Train into orbit," he said with bags of energy.

"Around Serothia?"

"Around Serothia and do you know what?"

"What?" she said smiling.

"You're going to come in handy after all, would you like to help me?"

"Yes Captain!"

He staggered back at her enthusiasm. "Good," he said. "That trap door there, see it?" He was pointing to the floor that was in between the engine room and the other part of the Train. There were apparent cracks in the floor and she could see a little lever that was folded down flush with the floor.

"Yes," she said.

"Right, pull the lever, and underneath the floor, there's a stash of Carnane fuel. I need you to take this shovel," he pulled out a big spade from behind the controls in a corner of the room that Evie hadn't seen before, "and shovel some of it into that furnace."

"What furnace?"

"Underneath here," he was standing at the central control panel. He pressed a button and an electronic door opened right in front of her at about knee height. Suddenly, her legs felt extremely hot—burning hot.

35

"That's a furnace!" said Evie.

"Yes, now open the door. You'll have to use the mitt because it's very hot."

After finding the mitt he was talking about, Evie opened the door to the furnace, and then opened the trap door to the stash of fuel and underneath the floor, she saw a large chamber filled to the brim with what looked like coal. Only this was glowing, like the pieces scattered around on the road were glowing. The individual pieces glowing on . . . and off, on and off.

"Quickly, quickly, there's no time to waste. We need lots of heat!"

"It's like it's a steam train," said Evie.

The Captain just smiled and returned his attention onto the front controls looking outward onto the planet below.

As soon as a shovel full of coal was tossed into the furnace, Evie would lose sight of it but the blaze inside would stir and hiss and grow bigger and hotter. She had done three or four loads.

"How much do I need to shovel in, Captain?"

"Er . . . that should do it, that should do it. You can close the furnace door now."

And so Evie put down the shovel, picked up the mitt again and closed it, and then also closed the trap door. The Captain pressed the same button as before and the outer electronic door to the furnace closed and she was no longer in the line of direct heat.

Evie then stood back and watched the effects of what she had just done. The fire, (or whatever it was in the furnace), had been blazing violently and she followed the thick metal pipe with her eyes all the way up to the ceiling, and she wondered what it was all for.

"Ah! We're in orbit!" said the Captain.

"We didn't have to go through all that to get in orbit around the Earth."

"No, Earth doesn't have nearly the amount of defence barriers around it than Serothia has. We just managed to get through them."

"Defence barriers? But doesn't that mean we'll be detected now or something?"

"Probably."

"But they probably want to keep people out."

"Well of course, why else would you worry about putting up defence barriers?"

"But they might think we're hostile!"

"It's alright, we have a force field around us, not much can get through that. Least of all, any sort of primitive weapon found on Serothia. And I notice you said *they*. Have you been space travelling before?"

"Of course not, why?"

"Well it's just that *usually*, someone new to space travel doesn't believe there's life on other planets."

Evie was quiet for a few seconds. "I guess . . ." she said timidly, "I guess I read too many science fiction books."

The Captain smiled.

"What did you need all the heat for anyway? I mean, how exactly did the heat get us into orbit?"

"It didn't."

Just then, there was a *ding!* from one section of the central control deck.

"Ah!" said the Captain, "nice cup of tea!"

Evie frowned, "The heat . . . makes *tea*?"

He picked up the most perfect looking cup of hot tea, and then picked up a second one—both from some other part of the control deck that Evie hadn't noticed before.

He extended the second cup to her and said, "What's wrong with that?" He took a sip of his own.

She took the cup offered to her, eyes fixed on the cup, infuriated. "You mean . . . I shovelled that coal into that furnace, like a last poor frantic soul on a sinking ship, puffing and sweating like some poor forgotten sod in an engine room . . . so that you could have a cup of tea?!!"

"Not at all," he replied calmly, "that would just be cruel. No, it's the *steam* that gives the Train the thrust it needs, not the heat. The heat it creates is just an added bonus—boils the water. May as well have a cup of tea while we're working eh?" He took another sip.

". . . So, now we're in orbit . . ."

"Thanks to you."

Evie looked relieved, and she too took a sip.

There was some white noise that suddenly filled the room, and then some crackly snippets of voices and music, as if someone was tuning a radio.

"Hullo,' said the Captain to himself, "what do we have here?" He walked with his cup over to a corner of the room that was next to the wide window. "My radio communicator's picking up the signal on this planet."

"Like a radio station?"

"Sort of. Only I've heard that Serothia only has one station. Radio, television, iStream, everything."

"So everyone's always watching and listening to the same thing?"

"Precisely."

"But what about people with different tastes?"

"Well everyone could have the same taste, I don't know."

"You've never been here before?"

"Yes."

"You have?"

"No. I mean *yes*, I've never been here before."

Evie looked worried.

The Captain just smiled and said, "Exciting, isn't it."

Evie's eyes wandered across the front control deck. "Erm . . . Captain?"

"Mmm?"

"That dot on your radio scanner is getting awfully close to the middle, what does that mean?"

"Well it just means that whatever the dot *is*, it's getting closer to us. The middle point there, is us."

"Isn't that bad? It's moving awfully quick."

"Quick*ly* Evelyn, you really must learn some basic . . . shooting star that's moving quick. It's so close, we should be able to *see* it!"

"Captain! Look!" shouted Evie as she saw what was now coming into view out the window.

"It's the satellite. It's coming this way."

"And we're moving towards it!"

"Yes I *had* noticed that."

"Well what are we going to do? Can't we get out of its way?"

"I can't, we're both locked into orbit. It would take at least another minute to pull free. We don't have that long."

"We're going to crash!"

Evie couldn't watch. She was thinking twice now about her hasty decision to stay on the Train with the Captain.

Chapter Five

Satellite SB-17

The two vessels were soaring towards each other. The satellite, much bigger than the Train.

"Why doesn't the satellite do something?" shouted Evie.

"Because it can't see us. They'd be able to detect us, but . . ."

"We're invisible," she said, feeling that all hope was lost.

"Hold on tight Evelyn, I'm going to perform an emergency dematerialisation!"

The strange electronic windows tinted to black, the Captain lurched at a lever on the control deck and there was a big jerk and the roaring sound of the machinery. The steady *chuff choofety chuffing* kept pounding along in the background like a heart beat keeping Evie conscious and alive. Then suddenly and unexpectedly, everything stopped and Evie panicked (because of the whole heart beat analogy). But when she looked up at the Captain, who was flicking multiple switches and controlling the steering wheel, while at the same time holding a button down with his foot, she strangely found confidence in him. Although he appeared to be struggling, he looked like he knew exactly what he was doing.

And now when she strained her ears to hear, she heard a faint *chuff choofety chuff choofety chuff choofety bang*. And then there was a loud thud and the chuffing became louder until it eventually stopped altogether. There was silence and then one big puff sound from the steam that had built up in the metal pipe as if the Captain's Train exhaled a huge sigh of relief.

"We've landed," said the Captain.

Evie hadn't been expecting this. "Landed? Where?"

"Hopefully, in a nice convenient spot on the satellite."

"That satellite? But I thought that . . ."

"All I did was dematerialise and then just as the satellite passed our position, rematerialised. Always more preferable to crashing into something, don't you agree?"

"So we're inside it?"

"Yes. Want to come and see?" The Captain was already halfway to the door. He had grabbed an old brown coat and put a few items in its pocket such as a handkerchief, an apple, a small book, and some sort of tool that Evie didn't get a chance to see properly. "Well, coming?"

"Yes," she said finally, making a move towards him.

"Ah first, could you just switch my radio communicator off?"

The crackly radio station was still trying to get through until Evie walked over to it and found the 'off' switch. Then she went back over to join the Captain.

"And just hand me the rest of my cup of tea there would you?"

Evie came back with his cup.

"Don't forget to finish yours."

Evie went over and gulped down the last bit of her tea.

The Captain finished his off and put the cup down on one of the sofas. "Well come on Evelyn, we haven't got all year."

She quickly put her own cup down next to his and ran after him.

He stopped again and she bumped into him.

"And do your shoelace up."

The Captain had stepped outside while Evie was still doing up her shoelace. And when she was finally ready, she stepped off the Train and stood right beside the Captain. She looked all around her, yet again amazed by what she saw.

"So this is a satellite, huh?"

"A very large one at that. Satellite 'SB-one seven'."

"How do you know that?"

"Oh it's a . . . little skill I picked up in school, I assumed you would have as well."

"Huh?"

The Captain pointed to a part of the wall near them which had printed on it *Satellite SB-17*.

"Oh," said Evie. "Reading. Yes I learnt that at school too. That's *one* thing we have in common at least." Then she wandered a metre or so away, "I thought satellites were small and pokey, only enough room for someone to sit in a chair and the rest of it all just mechanics and stuff or whatever it is."

"You've possibly only seen Earth satellites. You saw this one from the outside, it was pretty gigantic. It would dwarf the Earth satellites that were around in your time."

"Are we in the future?" she said excitedly.

"No, we haven't travelled in time. Serothian technology is ahead that of Earth's, that's all."

"I thought you said they had primitive weapons."

"Oh their *weapons* are primitive, because they rarely have the need to use them. Therefore they haven't discovered the possibilities of improvements for them. They think that what they have now is sufficient . . . so I've heard."

Evie hesitated to ask the question, "Is James here? And Lisa?"

"What do you think 'SB' stands for?" he asked.

Evie had asked the question so quietly; the Captain had not heard her. It caused Evie to chicken out of her question and she joined him where he was in front of the wall that had the satellite's name on it. "Satellite, Serothia . . . Summer Camp . . ."

The Captain turned to her, "Summer Camp?"

She shrugged, "Just remembering how I got into all this."

"*B* . . . base, big," the Captain was guessing, "ballroom, battleship, Bing Crosby . . ."

"Captain . . ." said Evie, a little worried.

"Barricade, battlement . . ."

"Captain, there's someone coming!"

" . . . Boat, boundary, border . . . Bob . . ."

Evie was tugging at his sleeve. "A person!"

"Person? Person doesn't start with . . ." he turned and saw.

There was a figure—looked like a man, wearing a sky-blue jumpsuit and an opaque helmet stomping towards them. He had a big chunky gun in his grasp and he was aiming it at the two intruders—Evelyn and the Captain.

He finally stopped and now that he was standing right in front of them he was shorter than what they thought he'd be. This however, did not make him look any less tough.

From behind the black helmet, the man spoke, "Who are you and what business do you have aboard SB-17?"

The Captain raised his arms up in the air, and then nudged Evie so she'd do the same. "Well I'm the Captain and this is my friend Evelyn."

"We've come to get our friends!" said Evie.

The Captain shot her a glance and frowned.

The man pointed his gun right at Evie and she gasped in fear.

The Captain brought his hands down and pushed the man's gun aside. "Do you mind not pointing that thing at my friend?"

"Put your hands up and don't move!"

The Captain did as he was told, but he could tell that the man in front of him was a nervous wreck. His hands were trembling and he raised his voice terribly unnecessarily.

"Well what do you propose to do now?" asked the Captain, "stand there holding a gun at us until we finally crack and give ourselves in?"

"Just . . . you be quiet," he said, ". . . and come along with me." He circled around them so that he was behind them pointing the gun at their backs. "Now walk."

"Well you'll have to give us directions as there doesn't seem to be anyone else here to escort us."

"Be quiet!" he shouted. ". . . um, straight ahead . . . and then to your left."

"Right, let's get one thing quite clear," whispered the Captain to Evelyn, "I do all the talking alright?"

"Alright."

". . . then turn right . . . into that room. Quickly!"

The Captain and Evelyn complied and walked into a room with a long oval shaped table and many white oddly curved chairs all around it. There wasn't much else in the room—just a box mounted on the wall near the door with controls on it. The man pressed one of the buttons and the doors slid shut.

"Is this where you interrogate your prisoners?" asked the Captain.

The man looked a little unsure of himself. You couldn't tell by looking at his face, because you couldn't *see* his face. It was in his body language.

"We don't have an interrogation room," he said defensively, "we've never had prisoners."

"What, not even once?"

"You are the first. Now kindly explain who you are."

"I already told you, I'm the Captain and this is Evelyn."

"The Captain of *what*? I know of no military base or vessel in all Serothia that should need such a rank."

"I'm the Captain of my own vessel, the Train if you must know."

"How did you get on board Satellite SB-17?"

"On my vessel, I would have thought that was obvious."

"I saw no vessel."

"Well that will take some time to explain. Time that we probably don't have. By the way what *does* SB stand for?"

"*I'm* asking the questions."

"Oh sorry, do please continue."

There was a pause. "Why have you come?"

"Well that depends on what's going on here. What *is* going on here?"

Pause. "Nothing. Nothing's going on here."

"Then why are you here all on your own? *Where is* everyone?"

"Everyone?" The man sounded worried.

"Well it's obvious this Satellite was built to have more than one person on board at a time, this place's huge. You've got a conference room by the looks, you've got loads of corridors, you've got—correct me if I'm wrong—you've got ample room for moving about in, multiple work stations and I wouldn't be surprised if there were even living quarters for all the workers. You are one of the Satellite workers I presume."

". . . Y-yes."

"Well where are your colleagues? Where are the security men? That uniform of yours doesn't look like a security uniform, so what are you doing dealing with a breach of security?"

There was a brief silence. "I'm a maintenance worker."

"How many people are meant to be aboard this satellite at any one time?" the Captain asked, leaning in closer to the man.

"Seventy personnel."

"And how many people are on board right now?"

"About fifteen hundred I should say."

Evie's eye's widened. This was not what she was expecting to hear. But when she saw the Captain's face, she could tell that it was exactly what he was expecting to hear.

"I should have rephrased that," said the Captain, "how many *workers* are on board?"

". . . One."

The Captain leaned in closer still and said in a low, calm voice, "I can help. I know there's something terribly wrong going on, and I can help you. But you have to trust me."

The man finally gave in his tough act. His shoulders relaxed and he rested his helmet in his hands for a short while but there was no less worry in his voice. "I don't know what to do. I've been alone up here for the last three months waiting for some help from Serothia. I've sent out messages and SOSs and no one seems to receive them."

Evie spoke, "Well we're not exactly from S . . ."

The Captain stopped her, "Well my friend, help has finally come. Sorry for the unexpected arrival but we're . . . undercover, so as not to create a panic down on the planet."

"Oh, understandable." The man reached to his head, grabbed onto his black helmet and finally took the thing off. "My name's Paulo Vistar by the way."

"He's just a kid," Evie couldn't help saying.

"I'm thirty-two," Paulo said defensively.

"I do believe Serothia's years are much shorter than Earth's," the Captain muttered so that only Evie could hear.

Evie thought he looked about seventeen years old, if he'd lived on Earth.

"It's very nice to meet you Paulo," said the Captain, "now I think you should show us to the main control deck."

The young man showed the two travellers into a spacious room with multiple control panels and work stations. The room was brightly lit and all the walls and desks and the floor were a gleaming white. On the far wall, was a huge window pane through which the surface of Serothia could be seen.

"This is the Bridge," said Paulo. "It's where most of the operating crew worked, and some of the maintenance team sometimes."

"What is this satellite's function?" asked the Captain.

"It's the broadcasting satellite," he replied with an air of surprise, "I thought you'd have known that."

"Oh well er . . . the base didn't give us a briefing, they just sent us up here."

"But everyone on Serothia knows about this satellite. It's how they get radio and television down there."

Evie said, "And so the *SB* would stand for . . ."

"Serothian Broadcasting. Listen, any ordinary civilian down there knows about SB-17. Where have you been living? In a cave?"

"Er yes, yes we have actually," said the Captain. "Tell me, if there are fifteen hundred people on board this satellite, where are they?"

Paulo looked hesitant to answer the question. He had a sort of dread of passing on the news look. But nevertheless, he did so. "They're down below, Captain."

"Down below?"

"That's where I've been keeping them," he said softly but was quick to jump in with an explanation, "because otherwise they would just get in the way and cause problems."

"But you have one *big* problem don't you?"

"Yes."

"All those people down there, they know nothing about this satellite and how to operate it."

"No."

"They're all confused as to how they came to be here and what this place is."

"Yes."

"And they just keep coming and coming and coming, one or two or three at a time."

"Yes!"

"And you don't understand why they don't know a thing about Satellite SB-17."

"No!"

"It's because, my dear fellow, they're coming from Earth!"

"Earth?"

"Yes, all those people are from Earth and they're getting trapped here for some unknown reason or purpose."

"There's actually a planet called Earth?"

"Paulo, when did all this start?"

There was a soft alerting signal from one of the control panels.

"Uh oh," said Paulo.

"Was it when you were first on your own, or before that? Or after that?"

"It's happening again," said Paulo.

"What's happening again?" said Evie.

"The teleportation process. The system is getting another replacement worker, I have to make the way safe." Paulo was racing around, first to where the alert signal was coming from, and then to a set of tall vertical transparent tubes at the far right side of the room. There were six of them, all standing in a row and Paulo was pressing buttons on what looked like a home security system near them. And suddenly, there grew a blinding light from two of the tubes, there was a buzzing sound, which became almost piercing, and then when the light faded, the group watching could just make out the outline of two figures—one to a tube.

It did not take long for Evie to realise, when the light started to disappear altogether, that the two people who had just appeared from nowhere before her eyes were her brother James in one tube, and her friend Lisa in the other.

Chapter Six

What It Was That Happened Because Of Whatever It Was

Evie gasped loudly and ran straight to the tube which contained her inanimate brother. He appeared not to hear her or even see her right in front of him. She called out his name a couple of times and then went to Lisa and called out her name. Her response was the same. Nothing.

"Why can't they hear me? Are they alright?"

Paulo put up his hand as if to quieten her, "Hang on, hang on. I mean *yes* they'll be alright, just wait."

Paulo was watching the two new comers, and reading his apparent relaxed composure, the others watched and waited as well.

Soon, the glass at the front of the tubes shifted around automatically to expose James and Lisa to the open air. Suddenly, their faces didn't look so lifeless. They both blinked out of their unconsciousness and soon looked stunned by their unfamiliar surroundings.

Lisa panicked suddenly. "Where am I?" she saw James next to her, "James? Where are we?" Then she saw Evie out in front of her standing in the middle of the room next to a tall man in a dark brown coat. "Evie! What's going on here? Where *is* here?"

James was a little slower in absorbing his surroundings. He liked to think things through, allow himself to get his head around something before exposing his emotions and thought processes. He also liked to think he was in control of a situation and so he tried very hard to think of something more intelligent to say than *what's going on.* But all he could manage when he stepped out of the tube cautiously was: "What's going on?" His eyes locked onto Evie's straight away.

Paulo took charge. He had done this many times before. "Now, just come this way, you two."

"Their names are Jake and Liza," said the Captain.

"James and Lisa!" said Evie.

Paulo had grabbed them both by the arm and started escorting them towards the corridor leading off the Bridge.

"Wait a minute," objected James, "I want to know where we are and how we got here!"

"You're on Satellite SB-17," said Paulo hurrying them along.

"But how . . ."

"You got here by some sort of teleportation," Evie said.

"Via a transmat beam I should think," said the Captain after having a brief look at the tubes and the controls near them. "Rather a powerful one to be able to transport people from Earth all the way out here."

"Are you mad?' cried Lisa. "Where is this?"

"There's no need to worry," said Paulo still pulling them along not wanting to delay what had become such a routine job for him. "Please don't panic. I'm just taking you somewhere where you can sit and rest and . . . well, talk to other people who are in the same predicament."

"You can't just cart them off," said Evie.

"Wait!" cried the Captain.

"What, you want them to stay here?" asked Paulo.

"Oh no, *that* doesn't matter, you can take them away and put them where you need to put them but there's one thing I need to know—urgently."

"Well I'd like to get these two . . . Evelyn, would you take them?"

"Take them? Take them where?"

"Evie, what's going on here?" James said. "what do you have to do with them?"

"Do you know these Earth people?" Paulo asked Evie, a little confused.

"Oh . . . no, no I don't." She gave a quick glance of warning towards her brother. "Well how could I? They're from Earth."

Paulo frowned—not quite satisfied.

"Where do I take them to, Paulo?"

"Down the corridor, take the first left and there's a ladder behind the door, you just turn the wheel to open it. Then once you get down, follow the passage along and put them in one of the big chambers along there."

"Right, got it. Come on then you two. Follow me."

James and Lisa, gob smacked, followed Evie without quite being able to speak.

Paulo came back over to the Captain's side. "Now what's this urgent thing you needed to know?"

"I'm up here to solve a problem, right?"

"I hope so, sir."

"And I need to know things in order to formulate a solution to the problem, right?"

"Well yes, a bit like algebra."

The Captain rather liked this analogy, "Yes, rather like algebra. What I need to know is this—and I need to trust you to be honest with me."

"Oh of course, sir."

The Captain stepped right in close to Paulo and put an arm around him, "What happened to the original crew of Satellite SB-17, mmm?"

That look of dread once again came over Paulo, and his eyes seemed to fill with a terrifying fear. "They're all dead, sir."

"Dead?" he said softly. "How?"

"It was horrible . . ."

The Captain walked over to a chair and sat down.

". . . the noises, the screams, the cries for help and I couldn't do anything because . . ."

The Captain inclined his head, listening.

". . . Because . . . I was too afraid. I was a coward, I wouldn't come out and help my colleagues because . . . well, I would've died too!" He hid his face in his hands.

"Paulo, just because someone's brave, doesn't mean they're never afraid of anything. Fear is not the same thing as cowardliness." He then leaned forward with his elbows on his knees. "What *was* it that killed them, Paulo? Was it a man? A meteor storm? . . . An animal?"

"A *creature* . . . some sort of creature. I never saw it . . . just heard it, saw the effects."

"But what did it do after the attack?"

"I don't know. I haven't seen anything unusual since then. I waited a long while and when there was nothing but silence, I came out of my hiding spot . . . and then I saw what it had done. I looked around everywhere—searched the whole satellite from top to bottom. Nothing around but dead men. No sign of life. No sign of the creature."

"And so then what did you do?"

"Well, I did what's meant to be done when a satellite worker dies or retires or stops working for whatever other reason—I tried to call others up."

"From Serothia?"

"Yes. There's a base down there you see that trains people up for the many different jobs up here on the Satellite. Operators, emergency navigators, news reporters, film crew, technicians, security men, cleaners and maintenance workers. When we need a replacement worker, usually one of the Operators sends for someone. The base down on Serothia prepares the person who'll be best for the job, that person packs some belongings, gets in uniform and into position. Then an Operator activates the transmat beam and they arrive in one of those tubes. As you can see, the set up allows for up to six people to be sent at a time."

". . . Yes . . . and so what went wrong?"

"Oh, oh . . . yes well, it was me you see, who was left to operate the transmat beam. There were things up here that were in desperate need of repair, the oxygen supply had been damaged and so I was losing oxygen every second . . . well what I'm trying to say is that in my urgency to bring more workers on board . . . I pressed all sorts of buttons, trying to get it to work. I mean, I wasn't trained to do that side of it, I had no idea how to operate it, I'm only a maintenance worker!"

The Captain was getting the gist, "And at the hands of an inexperienced makeshift operator, the system is accidentally sabotaged."

Paulo nodded, ashamedly.

The Captain got up and started examining all the controls closely. "I'd say what you did, was you tampered with the galactic coordinates changing them from the base on Serothia, to Earth. The computer wasn't given any specific coordinates of *where* on Earth, so it's using many different random locations and taking many different random people."

"Oh dear."

"And not only that, but you got the system stuck. It's only a computer after all, glitches are to be expected; and it continuously thinks that you need more workers. You fed information into it saying 'I need workers', so it's bringing you workers. And it will keep bringing you workers until someone tells it to stop."

"How terrible," he said, still hiding his face in his hand.

"I should congratulate you. It's quite an effort, you couldn't do that if you'd tried." He smiled to lighten the mood, try and make Paulo feel better.

It didn't work. Paulo just felt more ashamed. He felt responsible for trapping all those Earth people here on Satellite SB-17. As a matter of fact, he *was* responsible for trapping all those Earth people there on Satellite SB-17—but it wasn't his fault. He was doing his best, and you can only do your best—when it *is* just you.

"Look, try and calm down, Paulo, we'll figure this out. Together we can fix it."

"We can?" he said doubtfully.

"Yes of course we can. We'll get by with a little help from my friend."

"Evelyn?"

"She's not my friend."

"But you came here with her."

"Well I haven't known her long enough yet. Only just met her. She's sort of a . . . passenger."

"I see. She seems awfully young."

The Captain was still scanning all the equipment with his eyes.

"Do you think it can be fixed?" Paulo asked.

"Oh just about *everything* can be fixed in some way or another."

"Perhaps, but do you think you can fix *this*?" He attempted to get a straight answer out of him.

The Captain took another look and rubbed the back of his neck, "Yes."

"Oh if only we had just one or two technicians up here. What tools are you likely to need? I can fetch them for you."

"The only tool I'll need is this," he said pointing to his head. "This is a computer programming problem, not a physical electronic or technical problem. Just by pressing a few buttons—and the *right* buttons at that, I should be able to have it done . . . oh." He had pressed a button, and the lights went out. The room was in total darkness.

Paulo was losing confidence in the Captain. "I thought you said pressing the *right* buttons would fix it, sir."

"Yes alright, alright, I'm just . . . familiarising myself with this control deck." He pressed what he hoped was the same button he just pressed before. The lights came back on. "There we are. See, no need to worry."

James and Lisa had followed Evie out of the main control room known as the Bridge, and Evie was saying, "You mustn't act like you know me, I'm supposed to be from his planet."

Her comment was ignored for now and when they were well clear of the Bridge, James could finally ask the question he'd been dying to voice, and he asked it quite severely and in a rough raspy whisper. "Evie, what on *Earth* is going on?"

She nervously replied, "It's funny you should say that."

"What on Earth is that supposed to mean?"

"Funny you should say *that.*"

James grabbed her by the shoulders and forced her to turn around and face him. They were stopped in the middle of a corridor. "Evie, will you stop speaking to me in code!"

"Sorry, it's something I must have picked up."

"*WHERE—ARE—WE?*"

"Paulo told you. This is Satellite SB-17. It's a radio and television broadcasting Satellite and if you'd have cared to look out the window while you were on the Bridge you would have seen a big orange planet, which is called Serothia." Evie quite enjoyed knowing more than her brother for a change—being the one in control. "Serothia is in the constellation Coma Berenices, which contains the galaxy M64 or otherwise known as the Black Eye Galaxy, and we are seventeen million light-years away from the planet Earth." She gave a little smug smile. "Next question."

Lisa butted in, "I've got a question. Why won't you tell us the truth?"

Evie became a little more serious and sincere now, "I just told you the truth. You were teleported from Earth to here. I don't really know how."

"How did you get here then?" asked James.

"Oh I came with the Captain."

"The Captain? Which one was he? The one in the blue overalls or the one with the big coat and messy hair?"

"It's not messy hair, it's cool."

"So *he's* the Captain. Isn't he a bit old for you?" James joked.

"Come on, we've got to get to one of these chamber things Paulo was talking about."

"And then what?" said Lisa. "Oh *come* on Evie, quit the gag, how do we get out of here?"

"How do you suppose someone like me could set up a gag like this?" Evie looked around at the walls and towards the end of the corridor. She saw just the thing she wanted. "Here, come and look at this." She walked them to the far end where she'd spotted a porthole-shaped indentation on the wall. She found a little groove in the top of it and pulled down. *Yes, it worked.* It was like a solid blind which concealed the view beyond. But now that the blind was off, Evie's companions could see something remarkable.

Space.

Nothing below. Nothing above. And the beautiful nebula was just coming into sight.

Both James and Lisa's jaws had dropped and they'd fought for the place closest to the window to gaze out and see that it was no joke. The sight was so real, they didn't even think of accusing Evie of using a painted backdrop and lots of black sheets. No, they could not deny it, they were out in space.

"Do you believe me now?"

James and Lisa were both speechless. So Evie didn't need a response from them. She just smiled, not smugly, but kindly because she understood what was going through their minds. She was remembering what went through her mind when she first set eyes on outer space from a different angle. She walked back to where they were in the corridor and approached the door Paulo had directed her to.

"What's down here anyway?" asked James.

"I think it's where Paulo's put everyone else."

"Everyone else?"

"You're not the only ones to have been teleported here. Lots of people from Earth over the last few weeks have been teleported onto this satellite."

"And we've got to be couped up with them until we can get back home?"

"Lighten up, you might see someone you know."

They were climbing down the ladder now. It was very dark in this part of the satellite. Evie thought it seemed cold and damp as well but she reconsidered and decided it was probably her imagination.

They reached the bottom of the quite warm and very dry place and found themselves in a dark narrow passage. Down here, the floor and walls were sealed with concrete and the only available light came from a fluorescent tube at this end and the far end which looked about fifty metres away. Along the walls, either side was a door every now and then. These, Evie presumed, were the chambers. She wondered what they were for; because to her, this seemed to be the right place for jail cells. But surely they couldn't be that. She opened one of the doors by turning a wheel again, James and Lisa standing right behind her.

They were astonished at what they saw. It was a large room with concrete walls, floor and ceiling, one fluorescent light in the middle, no windows; with at least one hundred people all crammed in. Their presence in the doorway appeared to trigger a bit of a stir. After a short delay, someone stood up and asked of Evie, "Is it time? Are we getting out?"

The middle-aged man's question provoked more people to stand up or call out with desperation in their eyes with a flicker of hope. "Please, can we get out of here?"

"Have you come to save us?"

"Have you seen my mother? She's tall, greying hair . . ."

"Please, I need to get home."

"Are you in charge?"

"Are you responsible for all this?"

"Please, let us out!"

Evie covered her mouth and her heart filled with pity for all these people. Just as she was about to say something, she realised there was nothing she could say to answer their questions, and so she shut the door again.

She stared at the floor for a while with her back against the door. She was hit suddenly with the horrible reality of it all, and she was thinking *thrice* about deciding to come on the Train with the Captain.

"All those people have been teleported here just like us?" asked James.

Evie managed a nod.

"You mean, we're all stuck here just like them?" said Lisa.

Without replying, Evie walked a shortish distance to the next door, turned the wheel and opened it slightly.

From beyond, a similar sound arose from a mass of people within, and she quickly shut it.

It was the same with the next room and the next.

She then walked further along the passage skipping about six doors on each side and turned the wheel of another door. The three of them peered in and saw a huddle of about fifteen or twenty people. All of them looked up with the most gloomy expressions. Just like the others in the first room, they looked tired, hungry and desolate.

"Well," said Evie in a flat tone, "I guess this is where I drop you off."

"Drop us off? You can't leave us down here," James said.

"I guess . . . at least it's safe."

"What do you mean safe?"

"The Captain said . . . there could be danger. At least locked away you'll all be safe, I guess. That's why Paulo brought them all down here."

"What's happening?" asked one of the others already in the chamber. "Are we in danger?"

Evie felt so sorry for all of them. She wondered how long they'd been down here. "I'm sorry," she told the woman, "I don't know. But I think . . . I don't know but I think down here must be the safest."

The three of them came right into the chamber.

"Safe from *what*?" asked Lisa.

"I don't know," Evie replied with her head low. "All I know is that Paulo told me to bring you two down here. He's doing his best."

"How long have you known him?"

"About . . . ten minutes."

"How can you trust him?"

"I don't know," she said pleadingly, "but I do trust the Captain."

"I mean, have you people even been fed?" James asked the group.

"Oh yes, we get given puréed food every now and then. Not very much but it's quite nice."

"How long have you been down here?"

None of them could hear a single answer because fifteen or twenty people each called out a different length of time.

"What is this place anyway?" Lisa said softly.

"They look kind of like store rooms," James told her.

"Look, I'm really sorry I can't do anything to help you," Evie said slowly making her way back to the door, "but the Captain's going to fix everything and you'll be back home before you know it." She had backed into what should have been an empty space between the door frame, but instead it felt like the stomach of another person. She looked at the people in the room. James and Lisa were in front of her . . . so who was behind her?

"Where do you think you're going?" said a deep voice behind her.

She looked around and saw a large burly man standing in between her and her way out. He had been with the group a moment ago. She answered in a pitiful voice, "I'm g-g-going out th-there."

"I don't think so. *I'm* getting out of here." He stepped back out into the passage and reached for the heavy door.

"No!" Evie yelped, "James, help me! He's going to trap us in here!"

James ran to her side and put all of his weight on the door to keep it from closing, but the man was stronger than the two of them put together.

"Isn't that what you were about to do yourself?" James said while pushing as hard as he could.

Lisa saw a piece of long metal tubing on the floor amongst a pile of other rubble, so she grabbed it, ran over to the struggle at the door, took a deep breath in and clubbed the guy on the head—knocked him out. He came tumbling back into the room.

Evie quickly took her place just outside in the passage way.

"Evie! You can't leave us in here!" said James.

"I promise I'll be back!"

"You're no different from that guy!"

"He was just trying to save *himself*."

"Isn't that what you're doing?"

"But I could help! I've got to get back to the Captain. He'll have a plan!"

James softened his voice. "Evie, I don't even know who this Captain guy is, but what about the danger you said he mentioned. If you go up there you'll be in danger."

Evie considered what he said. Then she pictured the Train, and that nebula, and the Captain's face; then she looked at the people in the chamber. No, she definitely had to do this.

"I'm sorry, I've got to go back." She gave James a quick kiss on the cheek and slipped back out and closed the door before he had a chance to fight with her.

As she was running back through the passage way towards the ladder, she could hear her brother's voice calling, "Be careful!"

Then back inside the room, James slumped his head against the door and whispered, "Be careful."

Chapter Seven

Uninvited Company

The Captain heatedly banged his fist down on the control deck of Satellite SB-17 and made a short growling noise. Nothing was working. Any controls that appeared to be to do with the transmat mechanism would not function at all.

"What's the matter?" Paulo asked from one of the chairs across the room.

"What did you *do* to these controls, Paulo?"

"I wish I knew."

"Well whatever you did, you appear to have locked the teleportation mechanism. The whole system's stuck and I can't unstick it."

"So we *do* need a technician?"

". . . Yes. Unless I can short out the system but knowing which wires to pull would be like looking for a needle in a hay stack and even if we did manage to find them, I can't be sure of what other damage I might do."

"We've got to take the risk, surely."

He looked at Paulo, "Things like . . . short out the engine, cut off the oxygen supply, jettison one whole section of the Satellite, who knows? I'm not familiar with this control deck. Surely you know it more than me."

"Yes . . . but not much. I haven't had that many jobs on board yet you see. I could fix up loose wires, oil squeaky chairs but . . ."

The Captain nodded his understanding.

"I've already had a look at everything before you got here."

"Shhh."

"I'm sorry Captain, I feel like a failure . . ."

"Shhh." The Captain put a finger against his lips. "What was that?" he asked slowly.

"I didn't hear anything."

After a pause of silence, there was a distant long moaning sound.

Paulo's face went white, and his eye balls moved up to look at the Captain.

"I hope that's not what I think it is," said the Captain.

Paulo was quiet, but inside his head it was very noisy what with all the screaming and yelling, fighting and dying. And he himself was saying *no, no, no, not again, not again.*

The Captain stood up, reading that look of dread on Paulo's face, "Is that what I think it is?!" He towered over the boy in his seat.

Paulo looked up at him slowly. "The creature. It's still here, and it has woken up."

Evie stopped in her tracks when she heard the noise. It was distant, but very eerie. It was a low raspy groaning, and her imagination imagined the worst—as imaginations tend to do. It sounded very big, very mean, and very scary—hairy even . . . or maybe slimy. Then she told herself that it must have been an old pipe somewhere groaning because of its age or need of repair. She started walking again through the corridor towards the Bridge, and she heard it again. She didn't stop this time, she just quickened her pace and then eventually started running.

"This creature," said the Captain, "it killed everyone on board did it not?"

Paulo nodded, "'cep me."

"How did it kill them?"

"What? Sir, you've got a morbid curiosity."

"I need to find out everything I can about it. And it's 'Captain', you can stop calling me 'sir'."

"Well . . . Captain er . . . as I said I never actually saw it but . . . the way all those grown men were screaming, must have been pretty painful, and slow," he added. "And afterwards, they looked all kind of . . ."

"All kind of what?"

"All so . . . if I said lifeless, would you know what I meant?"

"Well . . . they were dead so . . ."

"No but, if someone had just died and you saw them straight away, you'd have to check wouldn't you—to see whether they were dead or not. Well, these poor souls . . . just looking at them, you knew they weren't alive. They were real pale . . . like they'd had all the life just drained out of them in just seconds."

Something occurred to the Captain. "Where are they now? I mean, they're not still lying around everywhere are they."

"No I . . . I had to move them. There were so many of them and I had to try and get to work. Plus, they were so horrible to look at all the time. So . . . they're in one of the store rooms now, down below. I suppose we'll have to jettison them or dispose of them somehow but I couldn't bring myself to do it."

There was another distant moan.

"Whatever it is we can do about that creature," said Paulo, "we'll have to do it fast!"

Just then, there were fast running footsteps beyond the Bridge. The Captain, wide-eyed, went over to the door and listened. Paulo, feeling more terrified and defenceless by the second bolted over behind the Captain. And so there they were, the two of them, lined up behind the door. Hiding. Waiting.

Then it burst in—a young girl looking about as frightened as them.

"Captain? Paulo?!" she said in terrified alarm. "Where have you gone?!"

"It's alright, we're here," the Captain sighed.

Evie sighed in relief as well, but still looked very worried. "There are noises coming from . . . somewhere. Please tell me it's just the plumbing."

"I'm sorry Evelyn it's not the plumbing," he announced.

"It's something very big, very mean and very scary," said Paulo.

"Paulo where did you hide from it last time?"

"Is that all we're going to do, just hide?" said Evie.

"For now. Where is it?"

"I'll take you, come on."

Paulo led the way out of the Bridge and down through the white corridor.

"It feels like we're going towards it!" Evie said.

"This way." Paulo turned right and then the next right was a small door, which he opened. It looked as though they were all climbing into the cupboard-under-the-stairs, and when they popped their heads in, they saw that it was a small alcove but with no floor. Instead there was a drop of about two metres with another one of those metal ladders leading down. Paulo closed the door behind them all and from that moment on, there was no light whatsoever. Evie could not see her hand in front of her face.

"Trouble is," said Paulo, "the thing probably knows there are still people on board, and if it doesn't catch anyone it won't stop looking. Last time, it got lots of people and so it wasn't to know it'd missed anyone. This time, there's no one else."

"All the people down in those chambers," said Evie, "what about them?"

"It can't get through solid wall. Otherwise . . . well it would have got me."

"Not if it didn't know you were here," said the Captain.

Paulo expressed a "huh?"

"What we need to know is whether the creature is sensitive to heat, or sound or movement. You see, if it isn't, it would not have known there was someone else on board and so wouldn't have come looking, and so wouldn't have needed to come through any solid walls."

"Oh that's really filled me with joy and reassurance," said Evie. "You mean, we might not be safe here?"

"I told you you might not be safe if you stayed on the Train with me."

That hit Evie hard. She knew she had no right to complain, for this . . . this was her choice.

It groaned again and this time, it was louder. Nearer.

"If only I knew more about it. What it wants, what it needs. What it *looks* like."

"And why it has come back," Paulo added.

"I'm more interested in why it went away for three months." Then he added, purely for Evie's benefit, ". . . Serothian time."

Mmmrrrreeeerrrrrgh. It's groaning was slightly louder again.

"You said it looked like the life was sucked out of them . . ." the Captain was thinking out loud. "Perhaps it wants the energy. All that energy that's constantly pulsing through the human body. Is there anything else you can remember? Any sounds it made or tracks it left?"

"No tracks . . . although come to think of it, the floor looked . . . I don't know, a little more polished in some areas. I just assumed it was an unfinished job of the cleaners. Bit damp as well—the floor."

Mmmrrrreeeeaaarrrrgh.

"It's getting closer," said Evie. "I wonder where it is."

"At a rough guess I would say around near the news rooms."

The words *news rooms* made the Captain think. "This Satellite, everything that's broadcasted to the planet, it's filmed and recorded up here is it?"

"Not everything. The news is, and we do a television show occasionally to show people what it's like up here—sort of a bit of an advertisement for jobs—make people want to apply for something and start the training."

"And it's broadcasted all over the planet?"

"That's right."

"So everyone receives it?"

"Well, people who have a television or radio or computer or iStream thingies."

"And they only ever get the one channel?"

"Yeah 'course . . . you should know all this, where have you been?"

"I told you, in a cave. Now, there must be lots of broadcasting stations spotted all over Serothia."

"Yes, they receive all the emissions from the Satellite and they also film things there as well and send signals back up. Then transmissions are beamed out into people's living rooms and offices and pockets all over the world."

Mmmrrrreeeeaaaarrrrrgh!

"How did that thing get *on* to the Satellite in the first place?" Evie said.

"I don't know," said the Captain, "but I want to know why." And with that, he shifted out of his position in the hiding place and the other two heard him grab onto the ladder.

"What are you *doing?*" said Paulo in whispered alarm.

"I'm climbing a ladder."

Before Paulo could ask why he was climbing a ladder, he had opened the little door letting blinding light stream in for a moment or two. Then the door thudded shut and it was black again.

"He'll get himself killed!" said Evie and lurched forward feeling for the ladder.

Paulo pulled her back. "No, you mustn't go out there. You don't know what it can do."

"But the Captain's our only chance of fixing this whole thing!"

Paulo kept silent for a short while, worried. Then he muttered, "I hope you know what you're doing, Captain."

The horrible groaning sound became louder for the Captain but he didn't look very phased by it. In fact instead of hiding and staying out of sight, it actually looked as though *he* was looking for *it* rather than the other way around. It groaned again and the Captain followed the sound. However, as he slowly made his way winding through various rooms and passages, the sound sometimes seemed further away. Then he started experimenting.♣ He jumped up and down on the spot and flapped his arms about as if doing an impression of a butterfly—a very bad one at that. He ran up and down the short length of passage where he was and then executed a half a dozen star jumps. And then, the groan was louder.

The Captain smiled. The creature had just answered a very important question for him. The creature was sensitive to movement or had exceptional hearing. He now proceeded onto his next experiment.♦ He put a hand up to his mouth and cleared his throat, like what you might do when waiting at a shop counter and the assistant is not paying attention and doesn't know you're there. Nothing happened. He cleared his throat again a little louder. Nothing happened, he waited. There was a big long moan again but it didn't sound any nearer from him. Then he shouted at the top of his lungs, "I'm over here!!!" and after a while, he heard another groan and this time, it sounded further away.

♣ It should be noted here that you should never do this if you are inexperienced at recognising, relating to, fighting or defending yourself against unknown alien species.

♦ . . . which again, is not advised.

He smiled again. Now the thing had told him that it did *not* have exceptional hearing, but was just sensitive to his movement. Paulo would have been very still when he was hiding in that tight spot—not so much by choice but because there was hardly any room to squirm about in anyway.

He then, very slowly and cautiously, made his way through the satellite towards the moaning which sounded quite regularly, conveniently.

"What's it heading for?" the Captain thought to himself. "Where's it going?"

"I'm worried for James and Lisa," whispered Evie.

"The new arrivals, why them?"

". . . and all those people down there with them. Everyone, I'm worried about everyone."

"I think you know them," Paulo said accusingly. "Do you know them? Well?"

Evie wasn't as efficient as the Captain at making up stories. She hardly ever had to do that particularly horrid duty because she was usually an honest girl at school and at home. So . . . she gave in. "I'm sorry Paulo, we haven't been honest with you. We are . . . I am actually from Earth myself. We're not spies or anything," she was quick to say, "and we *have* come to help. You can trust us. And you can trust us even more now that I've told you the truth can't you." She smiled to the blackness, and so Paulo didn't see it.

Paulo was silent for a moment which Evie found unnerving.

"You . . . were lying . . . before?"

"Well, yes . . . no. The Captain did actually. I didn't want to lie."

"I've never been lied to before."

"What *never*? Not even once, one little lie?"

"Is there such a thing as a little lie? A lie is a lie isn't it?"

"I . . . suppose so," Evie was in thought, "but I guess . . . a lie can either have a little or a big effect." She felt proud of that little thought.

"So you and the Captain are from Earth?"

"Well . . ." she didn't know where the Captain was from, but to keep things simple, she replied, "yes."

"But how did you get here, if you weren't sent from Serothia?"

"We came in a ship, a space ship. It's on board now."

"But I didn't see any space ship."

"Well . . . neither did I," she mumbled.

"It must be pretty small."

"It is I think. Anyway the important thing is, do you trust us still?"

"I suppose I shall have to, I have no other choice at the moment."

They heard the moaning sound again. It was louder and nearer again. Evie thought about the Captain and what he must have been doing. Was he alright? Were the people down in the chambers alright? The more she thought about it, the more worked up and panicky she felt about James and Lisa, whom she'd left trapped down there. *She! Evelyn Michelle Bamford* left her own brother and friend behind. The more she thought of *this*, the more she felt what a terrible thing it was to do.

"If that thing is sensitive to heat or sound or movement," she said, "then it'd definitely be heading for those chambers down there where all those people are. There'd be heaps of heat, movement and sound down there. And if it eats people to get their energy—what a feed! Hundreds and hundreds of people!"

"Evelyn, I hope you're not thinking of . . ."

"No one down there knows about this thing. They're probably terrified of the sounds."

"Evelyn, don't."

"And the panic would be creating more heat and movement and sound, only drawing it nearer!" She leant forward feeling for the ladder.

"No Evelyn, don't. It'll kill you as soon as it finds you." He grabbed her by the waist and tried to pull her down away from the ladder.

"You don't understand, Paulo. My brother's down there. And a real good friend. Those new arrivals—my brother James, and my close friend Lisa. And I left them down there."

"They'll be safe down there."

"You don't know that for sure."

"But what are you going to do?"

"I could warn them. Tell them all to keep quiet, I don't know. I can't stay here not knowing what could be going on."

Paulo couldn't catch her for the second time. She got to the top of the ladder, opened the door and it banged shut behind her. She stood still just in front of it for a while, trying to decide what to do. Then suddenly the door opened again behind her and Paulo came tumbling out. She helped him up and they both stood still in front of the door for a while, trying to decide what to do.

"This is a very bad idea, Evelyn."

"You can call me Evie by the way. It's much quicker."

"Okay Evie, what do you suppose we do?"

She whispered, "I suppose we talk very quietly, or better still, not talk at all."

Paulo mouthed the words *good idea.*

Evie had her mind set on going to the chambers down below but when she came to think of it, what would she do then? Hide down there . . . instead of in the cupboard.

Paulo tapped her on the shoulder and when she looked at him he was making shapes with his mouth—speaking with no sound coming out.

"*What?*" she whispered.

He rolled his eyes back, "If you want to get to the chambers, we'd better hurry, the creature will be on its way as well."

Evie wanted to get back in that little room and hide so desperately, but she also wanted so desperately to know that James and Lisa were okay.

Without another word, they walked briskly to the chambers. Evie didn't know the way from here, so Paulo led.

When they got closer and closer to the passageway leading down to the chambers, the noise of the creature got louder and louder. Evie's heart rate was getting faster and faster and Paulo's footsteps were getting quicker and quicker.

"Moving faster might attract the thing," said Evie worriedly.

"But it's coming this way already remember, if your theory is correct."

They had reached the door with the big wheel on it. Paulo opened the door and they climbed down the ladder. As Paulo jumped onto the hard floor, he said, "Which chamber did you put them in?"

"I don't know," she replied jumping down herself. "It was down a fair way, the one with only about twenty people in it."

As they were hurrying down the passageway, Evie had a thought, "Hey you said the creature wouldn't be able to get through solid walls."

"Yes . . . ?"

"Well what's to stop it turning one of these wheels and getting in the normal way?"

". . . Um . . ."

"They're not locked or anything."

"There's never any need to lock the store chambers."

"So?" she was panicking.

". . . Well maybe it doesn't have ordinary hands and fingers like us."

"You don't *know*?"

"No, that's just how I . . . sort of imagined it. I never actually saw it. Is this the door?"

Evie looked up and down the passage, then at the door, "Yes, I think so." She put her hands on the wheel of the door, but then heard a great big yelp from Paulo.

"Wait!!"

"What?"

"Once we're inside, we can't shut ourselves in."

"What?"

"There's no wheel on the inside, that's why all these people can't get out, you can only open and close the door from the outside."

"Why didn't you say that earlier?"

Mmmrrrreeeeaaarrrrrgh!!

They looked at the ceiling, hearing the nearness of the creature.

"It's right on top of us."

"We're not safe here!" cried Evie.

"We can't go back now, we'd run into it!"

"What do we do?"

"If we go in there, it'll get twenty two people instead of just two people."

"Assuming it can't open the door."

The two of them were dancing on their tip toes in a panic.

The creature was moving above them. Moving towards the door that led to the ladder.

"Did you close the door up there?" Paulo asked.

"No. Didn't you?"

"I was in front of you."

Evie's eyes showed that she'd lost all hope.

Soon enough, the two could hear a strange squelching sound coming from the end of the passageway where they had come from. And then the creature let out a long deep moan and this time, it was louder than ever.

There was a strange blue light coming from the entrance. Paulo and Evie knew they were just seconds away from seeing this creature with their own eyes, but they couldn't imagine what the blue light was about. It was moving, flitting around along the floor illuminating the dark passage and it became stronger and stronger, as the thing made its way down the ladder.

Then at last, there it was, about thirty metres away, nothing but bare, honest, blob-like muck.

"Is that what we've been so terrified of?" said Paulo.

Mmmrrrreeeeaaarrrrrgh!!!!

The sound just about shattered their eardrums.

"I think that's fair enough, don't you?!" said Evie, grabbing Paulo's hand. She started bolting along the passageway dragging Paulo along with her. "What's at the end of this passage?" she shouted.

"I don't know, I, I don't think there's anything."

The blue-light-pulsating blob creature of indeterminate shape started globbing and squelching after them at a surprisingly quick pace.

"Please don't tell me this is a dead end," cried Evie.

"I . . . think it's a dead end."

"Maybe you didn't hear me; I said tell me it's *not* a dead end!"

They'd reached the dead end. Inside her mind she was saying goodbye to the world. Goodbye mum, goodbye dad, goodbye James . . .

Mmmrrrreeeeaaarrrrrgh!!!!

"What are we supposed to do?!"

Paulo looked right at the monster that was still coming towards them and swallowed. "We die."

Chapter Eight

Don't Move

Evie looked to her right where there was another doorway to another chamber. "Maybe we could get inside and just hold the door shut."

Paulo shook his head. "That thing's far too strong. I heard stories from some of the workers of what they'd seen before they died."

"Couldn't we at least try?!"

"Look!"

The creature was no more than five metres away. Evie panicked and tried to get the very furthest she could away without actually dissolving into the wall. She saw Paulo in front of her and he looked faint—he was turning pale while trying to duck past the giant thing.

"DON'T MOVE!!" came a loud voice from the entrance end of the passage. It was the Captain and he was standing way over there completely still.

"Well don't just stand there, come and save us!"

"No, we all must stay absolutely still! Paulo, very slowly move away, very slowly, I don't want to see you moving, that's how slow you must be!"

"How am I supposed to do that?"

"Just do it!" shouted Evie.

The creature had slowed its own pace once the bodies in the passageway had frozen still. It now seemed to shift its attention onto the doors lining the passage.

"It's sensitive to movement then," said Paulo softly.

"The chambers, all the people in the chambers, it'll be after them," said Evie. "What do we do now?"

Paulo hadn't the faintest idea. "Wait for it to go away?"

"But it won't go away, not with all those people in these rooms moving around, not knowing what's going on."

Paulo could feel himself shaking, his kneecaps wobbling, and he dare not blink his eyes. He had been only a metre away from the creature at the point where the Captain had appeared and he had started to feel his energy being drained from him. He felt faint and short of breath just being near this thing.

It had now moved away however and squirmed more towards the entrance end where there were occupied chamber rooms. The observers could tell it was trying to cipher what needed to happen to get the door opened.

It pushed its slippery, slimy body against one of the doors. (Evie noticed it was the one next to the room where James and Lisa were—one further along to the right.)

She looked at the creature carefully and watched with dread what it was doing. The blue glary light that glowed from within appeared to be dancing around, swirling here, darting there; and as the creature pushed itself more against the door, its front seemed to gradually take on the shape of the wheel that held the door shut.

"I'm sure that thing couldn't get through a door like that, it's impossible," said Paulo to Evie over his shoulder.

The creature paused there for moment or two.

"It's stumped," Paulo said somewhat thankfully. He smiled, "A little primitive door like that and it's stumped."

Just then, the light inside the blob creature stopped dancing around and maintained a constant glow again, and suddenly, its stomach,* which had assimilated to the shape of the wheel, rotated clockwise, turning the metal wheel with it.

Paulo's jaw dropped. "It's opening the door," he said under his breath.

"He's opening the door," said the Captain to himself.

Everyone held their breath while it slowly but surely did what was required to get the door opened.

Evie could not stand watching it or thinking about it. In a few seconds, this creature will have its prey—will suck the life out of a hundred or so people—from Earth. They didn't ask to be here, they didn't choose to step onto a Train for an adventure. They had been minding their own business, going about their daily routines, and now they were going to die, just like that. Once that was done, the creature would move onto the next room, where it could sense more movement. And then the next and the next; until every moving thing on this satellite was dead. And there they would be, standing in this passageway

---

* . . . that is, the part of its body located in an area where you would expect a stomach to be

frozen still for the rest of their lives. If they moved, they'd be hunted.

Evie could see no way out. The Captain didn't have any smart manoeuvres this time. All he was doing was standing there. Well Evie couldn't just stand there when her brother was about to be eaten . . . or absorbed . . . or smothered by this horrible blob. She decided to slowly move towards the door where she knew James and Lisa were, which was quite a fair way, but she would have to be slow and patient if she wanted to stay alive.

As soon as she came into Paulo's peripheral vision, he said in a raspy whisper, "Evie, don't!

She could see that he was about to grab her as she moved past, so she then broke into a run to avoid his capturing arms.

The creature had just prized the door open when it seemed to notice Evie's movement.

"Evie no!" shouted the Captain.

She'd reached the door she wanted and quickly yanked at the wheel, opening the door. Those inside looked up at her and she wasted no time. "Everyone in here, all of you, you've got to stay still! Whatever you do, don't move!"

"What are you on about Evie?" asked James walking up to her. "And what's that weird noise we keep hearing?"

"I mean it James, don't move a muscle!"

The people inside the chamber next door had an open door before them and they could not believe their fortune. There was cheering and jumping around and many started racing straight for the door.

The creature then lost interest in Evie and headed back for the rush of movement just behind it. There was a woman in shorts and a tank top that came running out, a huge smile wiped across her face. As she came into the passageway and came face to sort-of-face with the huge blob creature, she screamed at the top of her voice. Her smile gone, the energy quickly leaving her body. The Captain found it so difficult to stay where he was. He was attracted to screams. A scream usually meant someone needed help, and he was more often than not able to provide that help. It was like an instinct that had developed in him over the years long ago and now, he was fighting to act against that instinct.

The poor woman's scream grew weaker and weaker. She was very soon as white as a sheet used for a ghost costume, she fainted and then the creature slithered over the top of her and stayed there a while, while others now in front were feeling faint and growing pale.

James had not obeyed Evie and now led a small group out of the chamber next door to see what all the noise was about. The creature was just blubbering off of the young woman now and moving on to the next set of victims. When James saw that white, lifeless corpse on the ground, he froze just as Evie had told him to.

The creature was having a feast. It was now sitting on top of three other people and when it moved along, Evie saw that it was a boy and two men of different ages—all white and limp.

Evie found where Paulo was standing and went and got him. She figured that with the feast the creature was having, it would not follow any other movement just now. She grabbed him and ran straight towards the creature—James and Lisa following.

"What are you doing?" they all asked (at slightly different times).

"Tell them not to move!" she said to them. And then she yelled out to anyone who was listening, "Don't move, do you hear. As much as you want to run away, don't move and it won't find you!"

The others said similar things. Some listened, others didn't. They were too busy trying to save their lives to save their lives. Evie ran right past the creature, trying not to look at the terrible scene, and she ran for the Captain.

"Captain, how can you let this happen?"

"Paulo, Jason, pop your head into all these rooms while the creature's pre-occupied and tell them not to move."

They did so without asking questions. James didn't even bother to correct the Captain for getting his name wrong.

"But those people," said Evie, "they're dying. And you call it a pre-occupation?!"

"All I can do is make sure no one else dies." He then continued to shout out to everyone escaping the chamber not to move. He left Evie and opened some of the doors himself doing the same as what he'd told James and Paulo to do.

"Evie, what is that thing?" Lisa said in absolute terror.

She was extremely distressed. "I don't know. But we were very lucky to get past it."

The Captain, James and Paulo were just returning and the Captain quickly shooed everyone behind him. "Quick, get up that ladder and head for the Train, I'll be right behind you."

"What are you going to do?" Evie said.

"Just do as I say."

Evie was scared. Paulo shooed the others up the ladder, "Quick, this way."

The Captain waited until they were out of sight, then he put his thumb and index finger under his tongue and blew a loud whistle. So loud that it actually stopped those people who hadn't taken his advice and so now everyone was frozen, except for the Captain. He started jumping around and running on the spot shouting, "Come on, over here! There's a juicy body here just bursting with energy! Come and get me!" He waved his arms around high in the air until the creature started moving from its spot. It wobbled its giant jelly-like body around and even though it did not have any eyes, it seemed to be looking straight at the Captain. Everyone present finally *got it*, and they stayed absolutely still, hardly daring to move their eyeballs to watch the lunatic near the entrance.

Over it slithered, closer and closer and the Captain judged that it was about time he started climbing the ladder. Once he was up, he saw that the creature had a bit more difficulty getting back up the ladder than down it, but sure enough, it still managed it eventually. However, it did give the Captain a good head start. He ran straight for the Bridge as he seemed to remember the door to it was slightly more secure than those of the chambers down below. He hoped he was right.

On the way there, he exaggerated every move, making them as huge as possible because he thought that four others who were running in the opposite direction would attract the attention of the blob more so than one person. So, he had to make up the movement of three extra people.

Evie, James, Lisa and Paulo could not hear anything coming after them. They heard a long *mmmrrrreeeeaaarrrrrgh!* but it sounded quite distant.

"Is that guy off his rocker?" said Lisa. "First he says head for *the train*, and then he makes that big . . . thing come after us."

"He was leading it away from all those people down there," said Evie.

"Well . . . okay, fair enough but . . . dergh, what a wacked weirdo telling us to get on a train when we're up here in space. Did he escape from some sort of hospital?"

Evie ignored her for now. "Paulo, where was it that you first found me and the Captain, how do we get there?"

"This way," he said, taking the lead.

Soon, Evie recognised her surroundings again as the first ever sight she'd seen of Satellite SB-17. But she could not see the Train. *Oh no*, she thought. *Here we go, Lisa's going to have fun watching me do this.* She outstretched her arms and felt for the hard metal surface of the Train.

"Um . . . what are you doing?" asked Lisa, starting to believe Evie had escaped the hospital with the man.

"Looking for something."

"Okay, I don't know about you guys, but I think we should find somewhere to hide and not move."

"We can do that in a minute," Evie said feeling around through the air. She hit something. *There it is.* She felt for where the door was, but then her tummy sank after trying to open it and finding it wouldn't open. "The Captain must have locked it," she muttered.

"Evie, what are you on about?" James asked walking briskly over, a little fed up. And before Evie could stop him, he walked right into the side of the Train, coming away with his hand over his nose.

"Are you alright?" she asked.

"What on Earth?"

"I think we should take the girl's advice," said Paulo, "and find somewhere where we can just sit still and wait."

"Wait for what?" said Lisa.

"The Captain to return?"

"Yeah, bringing that blob thing with him, no thank you. He's the last person I trust right now."

"He said he'd be right behind us," said Evie. "I think we can trust him, and we will have to wait. There's nothing else we can do." She breathed in and out. It was strange her being the calm one, the leader, the maker of decisions.

"Who said you were in charge?" said James suddenly. And then he said, "Did I just crush my nose on . . . air?"

The Captain reached the Bridge, and he offered up a prayer of thanks when he saw that the door had an extremely complex lock. He closed it, locked it and then put all the loose furniture and other items he could find up against it. He knew what this creature was and he knew that it was quite easily slowed down by obstacles. He then raced around the room looking for things that would move when they were switched on. He tied some items to the blades of a fan in the corner of the room and turned the fan on. He switched on the motor which operated the ejector-compartment for dumping broken or useless materials. Then he reached into one of his deep coat pockets and pulled out a fluffy toy puppy, which he upended, flicked the switch to 'on' and put it down on the floor, where it started a cycle of walking two centimetres, yapping five times, and doing a back flip back to its starting position. *I knew that would come in handy one day*, the Captain thought.

Mmmrrrreeeeaaarrrrrgh!!!

The sound made him jump, it was very near. So he then pulled something else out of his pocket—this time his inside jacket pocket. It looked like a small remote-control, but it had an aerial that he popped up. He pressed a button, and in the blink of an eye, he was gone—leaving the room filled with as much movement as he could create, and an annoying yapping sound.

"How long are we suppose to wait here for him?" said Lisa.

"As long as we don't move," said Paulo, "we'll be safe."

"I can't imagine where he would have gone to," said Evie. "That creature sounds a fair way away and I expect wherever *it* is, the Captain is."

Just then, the group all felt a tingly sensation across their backs. They all suddenly looked at each other, but no one said a word, so they had no idea what they were all looking at each other for.

Then, there came a voice. "What are you all doing sitting around out here? Why not go *in*to the Train?"

They all snapped their heads around and saw the Captain standing behind them with a remote-control-like device in his hand. He was mainly looking at Evie.

"You locked it, that's why. And how did you . . ."

"I locked it, of course . . . sorry. Anyway you all stayed still, that was very smart, well done."

Lisa stood up, "Do we get a medal each?"

The Captain patted the pockets of his coat and jacket, "Sorry, I don't seem to have any on me." But then he pulled out a key.

"What are we going to do now?" asked James. "Just sit here until . . . until that thing somehow . . . dies."

"I'm not. I'm going for a ride."

Evie looked at him and frowned.

"On the *train* I suppose," said Lisa with a slightly patronising tone, smiling and nodding.

"You're catching on, Lisa," replied the Captain with a genuine smile. Then he looked at Paulo with a serious expression. "Paulo, you're in charge up here. I've left a distraction for the Ogrimite but it probably won't fool him for long."

"Wait a minute? What's an Ogrimite?" asked Lisa.

"That's a pretty stupid question," Evie said.

"It is certainly not a stupid question, it's a very important question. There are no stupid questions, a question is a question. No matter how good or bad a question is, it is still a question and questions always need answers don't they?" He paused. "Well?"

"Yes," said Evie.

"So . . . what's a Ogmarite, whatever it was you said?" Lisa said.

"Ogrimite. It is the proper name for what you may have been calling *the thing*. They only have two senses, touch and vibration awareness, but they are very intelligent creatures. This particular one is a he, and within at least four minutes he'll either have worked out that the movement in there is not from living beings or he'll have managed to open the door. Paulo, I need you to keep everyone as still as possible. Prevent more deaths, and if you can, try and stop more people from arriving in those tubes!"

"But I can't I don't kno . . ."

"Jack is here to help you. Jack . . ."

"It's James."

"James, you look like a technically minded person. Do everything Paulo says, don't ask why. Evelyn and Lisa, help prevent more deaths from happening, you know what to do."

"But where are you going?"

"Down to Serothia's surface. I have an idea."

"But how will you get there?" Paulo asked.

He held up a key.

"Ah, your small spaceship."

The Captain pointed a finger to him and clicked his tongue. He put on his glasses and walked to where the door of the Train was.

Evie could tell he had opened the door as she saw a glimmer of light from inside.

"One more thing," the Captain said walking back over to Paulo. "Even though the Ogrimite is intelligent, it doesn't know a great deal about human beings, so if he's after you and you stop moving, he's not to know that you're still there, got it?"

Paulo nodded, but his eyes were filled with fear and doubt.

The Captain put a hand on his shoulder and said, "God be with you."

Then he strode back to the Train and walked in.

James, Lisa and Paulo's jaws all dropped as they suddenly saw no trace of the Captain. Lisa was now starting to question her own sanity—that *she* herself had escaped from that hospital and had forgotten about it.

The next sound that filled the room was a loud rattly *Choofety chuff choofety chuff, Choofety chuff choofety bang! Choofety chuff choofety chuff, Choofety chuff choofety bang!* The rhythm grew steadily quicker and quicker and Lisa frowned to herself, feeling her own words wafting back to hit her in the face as she realised, that the noise sounded incredibly like a train.

Chapter Nine

Plan, Almost

The Captain had sidled past the sofas in his Train and gone straight to the controls on the centre control panel. After firing up the engine, the Train dematerialised and was now hovering in timeless, spaceless time and space. He calculated the coordinates for landing on the planet below and tapped them into the controls. Then he pulled a lever and after a moment of smooth soft *choofety chuff*ing, there was a loud *choofety chuff* and then the engine slowly calmed down and stopped.

He had a small peek out the front window and thought to himself, *perfect landing.* "Pity no one was here to see it," he said out loud.

He fiddled with a few more controls, shut the window and then with big strides, he walked out of the Train and onto the land. He scanned the terrain with his eyes, observing an ordinary looking street with ordinary looking houses and other buildings on it. Ordinary little cars were parked here and there along the street and some quite common birds were singing here and there. It was quite a lovely day. Mid morning, he guessed. He then turned back to the Train, shut the door and locked it. He looked back at the town, took his glasses off and then spun back round to face the Train. There were hills, some short fat bushes, a few ordinary looking trees. No Train—beautifully hidden. But suddenly, there was a sound that he did not expect to hear.

It was a little timid voice, which cleared its throat and said, "Captain?"

He couldn't see anyone. But then again, was that a little head he saw ducking behind . . . then he saw her.

"You're not angry with me are you?"

"Evelyn, I told you to stay on the Satellite to look after your brother and everyone else."

The Captain could see all of her now. And then she came right round from behind the Train to stand with him.

"I just couldn't resist the opportunity to set my feet upon another planet. Different ground beneath my feet, different air going into my lungs. And just look at this place! What's with those really weird looking houses? And those little boxes all the way along this street . . . I guess you'd call it a street. And that bird-song, it's so unusual. And those trees—I've never seen anything like them in my whole life! All this alien stuff, being in outer space, it's incredible! Only . . ."

"Only what?"

"Well, it's this invisible space ship thing, I . . . I don't . . . it's weird."

The Captain put a hand on her shoulder and gently pulled her in close to his side so they were both facing where the Train was square-on. "Do you remember how I said the Train wasn't exactly invisible?"

"Yeah. But it's not exactly visible either."

"No it isn't. Tell me what you can see there."

"Do we have time for this?"

"Tell me what you see."

She blew out a puff of air so her lips vibrated. "Ah, some more of those strange trees, some thick grassy bushy shrubs, some hills in the background."

"Are you sure?"

"Of course."

The Captain then took a firmer hold of her shoulders and shuffled her to the right. Evie wondered what he was doing, and he insisted she keep her eyes on the scene. She watched and watched as she kept being shuffled a little way to the right and suddenly, as if it was being revealed by the drawing back of a curtain, she saw a small house on a hill in the distance appear in the middle of the scene right before her eyes. She straightened up, her jaw dropped and he let go of her shoulders. Why hadn't she seen it before? It was there now, clear as day. She walked back to her left, expecting the house to disappear again, but this time it stayed in her vision. She popped her head back and forth a few times, trying to work out what had just happened.

"Okay so is there a house there or not?"

"There is a house there. You just didn't see it before now."

"Huh?"

"The Train isn't invisible. You're looking at its surface right now."

"But it's like I'm seeing through it."

"Not through it, at it."

"Oh I get it; it's like a camouflage thing. Like those octopuses in the ocean that can literally change their appearance to look like their surroundings."

"Well, it's like a camouflage, but the Train isn't doing anything. It's your eyes that are doing the work. It's a special coat of paint I guess you could call it. It forms an optical illusion. When looking at it, your eyes will show you whatever you expect to see. If the terrain is a flat, bare plain, you'll see a flat, bare plain all the way across. If it's hills and trees and bushes, and the Train is parked right in front, your eyes will fill in the gaps."

She walked to the right again, "And so . . . because I didn't know there was a house there before, I didn't see it?"

"Exactly."

"And then I *did* know it was there, so I now expect to see it."

"Right."

"What do *you* see when you look out there?"

"I see hills, trees, bushes and a house."

"But . . . you, well we *expect* to see the Train now, don't we?"

"Yes, but the stuff is cleverer than that."

"Cleverer?"

"Well, I can't explain the whole thing very well because I didn't invent the stuff but, it acts against your desire to see the Train itself. You might catch a glimpse of its outline at unique times, but you'll never actually see it in its full physical form . . ."

Evie thought that was a shame. Then she was just thinking how the Captain seemed to be able to find it without having to wave his arms about in front of him like a pratt, until he said . . .

". . . Unless . . ."

"Unless what?"

He pulled his trendy glasses out of his pocket, beckoned her over with his index finger and then put an arm around her shoulder. He muttered very softly, "Would you like to see what she looks like?"

Evie quickly nodded.

He slid his glasses onto her face and watched her expression change.

In front of the hills, trees and bushes that were before her, stood what she thought was a beautiful shiny deep green, classic, literal steam train—at least, part of a steam train. At the front was the engine just how she'd seen them in pictures and movies, and behind this was one carriage attached. The whole thing rested on huge steam train wheels that would glide along a track and when she looked up, she noticed a tiny dent and scratch in the paint work that she guessed was her doing when she was over-arm bowling the lumps of coal at it back on Earth.

"Whoops, I'm sorry," she said. When she looked up at the Captain, she saw that he had put on his driving goggles. She could tell he was looking at his Train.

"It's quite alright, you weren't to know," he replied, knowing exactly what she was talking about.

She didn't have to vocalise her wonderment and admiration for it, because it was already written all over her face. And the next time she went to look up at the Captain, he was not there. She spun around and saw that he was already a good ten metres away and she ran to catch up with him.

"I wish you wouldn't sneak off and leave me behind like that."

Without taking his eyes off where he was going, he replied, "I'm sorry, you'll have to get used to it, try and keep up and never go wandering off. I'm not used to having a companion with me all the time." He suddenly stopped, once again causing Evie to bump into him. "In fact, let's make a few rules. Rule number one, stay with me. Rule number two, don't wander off. And rule number three, as I said before, let me do the talking. How's that sound?"

"Stay with you, don't wander off, you do the talking. Got it," she smiled.

The Captain gave a nod and then continued his walking.

"Where are we going?"

"Rule number four, don't ask *too* many unnecessary questions."

"I thought you said there were no stupid questions."

"No *stupid* ones, but there are such things as unnecessary ones. A lot of the time questions are answered by the simple process of waiting and seeing."

Paulo, James and Lisa were still standing in the place where the Train had taken off. Paulo was left wishing that the Captain had left some more specific instructions for him. Like, for example, how to get onto the Bridge, how to stop the Ogrimite from getting through all the doors and, how to keep one thousand five hundred people completely still all at the same time. He couldn't believe the Captain had told him to try and stop more people from Earth being beamed up into the Satellite when he'd just recently been telling him he'd already tried tampering with those controls and failed superbly. He then thought of James, and how last time he did not have a companion, and now he did. James could be the source of great knowledge and skill. His hopes for this Earth-man were suddenly creeping up higher and higher fast before he could stop them, and he almost dreaded to ask him the question in case the hopes came plummeting down on top of him and he lost his will to survive. Nevertheless, being an efficient maintenance worker, that was the next thing he did. "James. I could do with your help trying to repair the transmat device. Do you think you could?"

James had to first come to a realisation that Paulo was talking to *him* before he could answer. "Me? No I don't know *anything* about transmat devices."

"It's simple matter transfer."

"Matter trans . . . we don't have that, I mean . . . we don't do that on Earth. At least, I don't."

"It's not like everyone on Serothia does either. It's very expensive."

"But," James felt he needed to reiterate, "I don't know anything about it."

"Don't rule it out. At least, not before you've had a look at it. The Captain said you were technically minded."

He stuttered to get a contention back, but Lisa butt in. "But how can we even move around with that creature after us?"

"I don't know," said Paulo looking at his watch. "But a whole minute's gone. And you know what the Captain said. In four . . ."

"Hang on a sec," said Lisa suddenly. "Where's Evie gone?"

Paulo shrugged slowly.

"What if she went on ahead?" Lisa panicked.

"No, there's only one way back into the corridors," said Paulo, "we would have seen her."

James turned and looked at the empty space behind them. "She must have gone with the Captain . . . somehow."

"But he just . . . disappeared, into thin air."

"We can't waste anymore time!" Paulo stressed. "The Captain said four minutes until that thing moves again."

"That's it!" said James. "We wait until the thing is back on the move—when it's fed up with the distraction the Captain set for it. Then we head straight for the Bridge."

"But what if it found a way through the door?" Lisa said.

"I can't see any other way, we have to risk it."

They heard a mighty groan from the creature a little way away.

"Come on, it sounds like it's moving back to the chambers."

The three, led by Paulo headed for the Bridge with a brisk walk and when they reached the corridor leading to the Bridge, they saw a blue glare coming from just around the corner.

"Freeze!" Paulo shouted, and they all became statues.

Lisa was afraid to breathe in case the Ogrimite would detect her chest gently rising and lowering. The blue light became stronger and its ray was creeping along the ground closer and closer. Then soon, they heard it cry out in its usual voice.

Mmmrrrreeeeaaarrrrrgh!!!!

It was so close; they should have been able to . . .

There it was. Gliding along the floor right in front of them. Its slimy, blobby body almost slithering against James' chest.

As he was beginning to feel quite faint, under his breath, he muttered the words, "Jesus, Jesus, Jesus."

Paulo and Lisa were relieved when they saw the creature pass them, but the next thing that happened, they had not bargained for. James suddenly lost consciousness, his body went limp and he clattered to the ground as if all the bones had been removed from his body. Lisa gasped and went to kneel over him but Paulo shouted out "No Lisa, don't move!"

It was James' body collapsing to the floor that made the creature come back. Lisa could hardly stand it. Her instinct was to run! Scream and then run for her life. But sitting still for her life? Who ever heard of having to do that? The adrenalin in her body was pumping and running around like mad. Being planted on the spot made her feel like she was going to explode.

When Paulo had frozen, he was looking right at the monster, and he daren't move an eyeball away from it. He stared and stared and stared at it and eventually, as if it had lost the staring competition, the creature sludged away.

When Paulo had felt it safe to move his mouth, he said, "It'll only attack a moving object."

"Yeah but, it got some energy from James just then. Will you help me?"

Paulo slowly moved over to them and knelt down with Lisa. They managed to wake him up quite quickly and James said that he had felt so weak and must have blacked out before hitting the ground. "If it was as intelligent as that Captain dude said . . ."

"Yes I know. Get close to your prey until they faint, forcing them to move and then . . . wallop, he can get you. Quite a clever trick he's got there, but he doesn't know it."

"I have a funny feeling he'll work it out though," said Lisa. "Eventually."

"Funny?" said Paulo, puzzled, "this is far from funny."

"No I don't mean funny ha-ha, I mean funny as in . . . horrible." Lisa frowned at her own use of words in puzzlement. *What stupid things we say sometimes,* she thought.

"Come on, let's get to the Bridge," Paulo said standing up.

"That thing will find its way back to all those people underneath us soon," said James. "Surely so many people can't all be frozen this whole time."

"Well . . . hopefully as soon as they see the Ogrimite again, they will freeze."

"But how long can we play this game with it though?" said Lisa worriedly. "I have a *horrible* feeling, it won't last long."

The Captain was walking briskly down one of Serothia's streets with Evelyn jogging just behind him, trying to keep up with his huge long strides.

"So just what is your plan down here on Serothia, Captain? Or is that an unnecessary question?"

"Certainly not, it's a very important one. My plan, is to find a broadcasting centre and see if my theory is correct."

"Your theory being . . ."

"That Ogrimite on board Satellite SB-17 must have a purpose for being there. And what is the purpose of the Satellite? To provide for the Serothian people all their local, national, international and intergalactic news and entertain them via the television or radio."

"Or iStream."

The Captain looked at her as if she'd said something really ignorant. But then he just said, "Yes," and kept on walking.

"So . . . you were saying."

"Well my theory is that the Ogrimite is going to try and use the Satellite to make a broadcast of its own. They look like very dumb and useless creatures, yet they have some very high ambitions and can become very power-hungry."

"What is it going to broadcast?" Evie said somewhat excitedly, as if she was sitting legs crossed in front of a teacher's chair on the carpet in a classroom, listening to the story of the day.

"Well I don't know for sure, but I have a shrewd idea it'll be something along the lines of *everybody obey me or you will die.*"

Evie was stunned. She stopped jogging. "Really?"

The Captain stopped too. "Yes really. I'm not one for sarcasm."

"It wants to take over the world?"

The corners of his mouth went down, his eyebrows went up and he swayed his head from side to side. "Er, well to put in simple terms, yes." And he started walking again.

To Evie, this sounded just like one of her science-fiction stories she often read. She muttered under her breath while taking off again to follow the Captain, "Unreal."

The small party had reached the Bridge and they had heard a couple of loud groans from the monster and then a quieter one.

"Those people down there are in trouble," said James, "I just know it."

"I know," said Paulo heading for a control. He flicked a switch and immediately, through an intercom speaker, mutterings and nervous mumblings could be heard. "We'll be able to hear what's going on down there."

"Can we talk to them?"

"Only if someone turns the speaker on down there, and they won't know to do it. Anyway, here's the transmat controls. This section," Paulo was showing James around, "apparently is to do with the galactic coordinates for place of origin, a-and this section, is the controls for actually activating the transmat."

James' expression was blank. His head was blank, he had absolutely no ideas. Paulo was beginning to lose hope just by looking at his face. James thought he'd get down underneath the control desk to see if there was *anything* at all he recognised. He was lying on his back looking up at the wires and labels, lights and controls. Then there was an alert signal. James hadn't touched a thing.

"Oh no," Paulo said rushing to the transparent tubes over the right side of the room.

"What does that noise mean?" Lisa asked stepping over a little toy puppy yapping away on the floor.

"It means we're getting more visitors." Paulo pressed some buttons by the tubes.

"You're letting them through?"

"If I don't do this, they get stuck between the two places in millions and millions of tiny atoms."

"Oh," Lisa merely said.

"Good thing you're here then," James said from under the control panel. "If it wasn't for you, Paulo, we'd be in millions and millions of tiny pieces, Lisa."

Paulo's job was finished and he stepped back to watch. This time, only one tube glowed with light, and when it faded, a little girl was standing there. Lisa gasped and covered her mouth. Paulo closed his eyes and puffed out a sigh of disappointment.

He greeted the girl by saying, "You don't happen to know anything about matter transfer controls do you?"

She looked around her and screamed, "Mummy!"

Lisa went to her. "Oh, poor thing."

"Where my mummy?"

"She's not here."

"I want mummy!"

Paulo stamped his foot in frustration. "James. Anything?"

He shook his head. "I can't make head nor tail of these controls. I come from a completely different planet, man!"

There were suddenly screams from the intercom.

"Oh no," said Paulo rushing over.

The screams were accompanied by a big groan of the Ogrimite.

"It's found them," Lisa said.

Paulo started jumping and running around the room. "Come on! Move around, we've got to distract it!"

"But it'll just come and get us!"

"It'll give everyone more time. Shut that door, we can assume it couldn't get in last time."

So the three of them did what Paulo was doing. Lisa tried to make it sound fun and care-free for the little girl. "Come on, let's do a dance and see if Mummy comes."

The sounds on the intercom speaker eventually became quiet—and this time, absolute silence resounded.

"We've done it," Lisa said puffing.

"Okay, we should be able to stop, our natural movement might be enough now," Paulo said.

They waited. James continued his useless task of looking at alien technology, Lisa continued trying to amuse the child, and Paulo walked to the door to listen.

They heard a slightly louder *mmmrrrreeeeaaarrrrrgh!* and then a louder *mmmrrrreeeeaaarrrrrgh!!* but then a quieter *mmmrrrreeeeaaarrrrrgh!* and then an even quieter *mmmrrrreeeeaaarrrrrgh.*

"He's going back down there," said Lisa panicking.

"No, no, I don't think he is," said Paulo.

And Paulo was right. The creature was moving in a completely different direction from before. He had managed to find a few more sources of energy—quite a sufficient serving. In fact, just perfectly sufficient to start his job. He headed for the news room. Where there was all the equipment he needed to send a brief but important message out to all the people on the planet below.

Chapter Ten

Square Eyes

Evie had followed the Captain down several streets for the last seven minutes with this question in her head. She had asked the Captain this question many times in her mind, but wasn't sure if she should actually say it out aloud. Deep down she felt she had a solution to the Captain's immediate problem, but in her mind it seemed so obvious that she thought the Captain *must* have already thought of it, had already decided against it and already progressed further in the problem-solving process.

They had passed many houses—presumably with people living in them. They were small square stone buildings all situated in a neat line along the street. They looked small from the front, but when one took the time to notice, the buildings were long. They didn't have much width, but a lot of depth, and so the streets were lined with long rectangle, sometimes curved boxes—all sprouting out from the dry and dusty road.

All these houses, Evie was thinking, *they must have people in them. People who would know where the nearest broadcasting station was.* This question kept on nagging at and bothering her. So she asked it.

"Captain?"

"Mmm?"

"Well I was just wondering. Couldn't you . . . I mean with all these houses around, couldn't we just . . . ask somebody. Save some time wouldn't it?"

Evie expected a remark like *I'd already thought of that, no we can't because blah blah whatever whatever.* But he spun around on his heels to face her, took a glance at all the flat, parallel buildings, paused and then said, "Well, if you want to go for the obvious."

Evie turned and walked straight to the first door she saw. The Captain was surprised at her eagerness and he followed her to the doorstep. She had already knocked on the door, and when the Captain came beside her he silently, with a gesture of his hand, reminded her, *I'll do the talking.*

She nodded agreeably and just then a woman opened the door. Evie might just as well have been on Earth, the woman looked just like your regular average old fashioned house wife. She had a pinny on and everything. With a floral design on it.

"Yes?" she said with a warm smile.

"Hello I'm Captain Johns and this is Evelyn, how do you do?"

"Well thank you."

Evie started, "We were wondering if . . ."

The Captain finished, putting a hand over Evie's mouth. ". . . you know where the nearest broadcasting centre is."

"Oh won't you come in?" the woman said.

"Oh, how kind of you, thank you very much." The Captain took a step through the door.

Evie gripped onto his coat and muttered to him so only he could hear. "Do you think we should?"

"Why not?"

"Well, she's a stranger. And why would she want to invite us in?"

"Evelyn, you must remember the people here are peace-loving and kind. You should be able to trust them with your life."

"I'd rather not have to. Anyway, we don't have time to stop do we?"

The woman cut in here, "It's just that my husband probably knows how to get there. You're better off talking to him."

"Ah, thank you," said the Captain and walked right in, taking the lady's invitation.

Evie cautiously followed.

"He's just down the back end of the house at the moment, hanging up a picture for me. Shemas! Shemas, come out here, there's someone who wants to see you."

The room they had come into (the first room of a long line) was what looked like a living area. A few lounge chairs, unusual looking upholstery designs and ornaments around the place, and in the corner, a television with a huge perfectly square flat screen.

Evie found herself looking at it. It was because it was *a television on another planet* she supposed, but much the same as at home. The Captain and the woman were talking in the background and soon she thought she heard another man's voice in the conversation as well. Then she felt the woman come and stand next to her—also looking at the T.V. screen. There was nothing really on, just a wonky picture with a bit of white noise coming from the speakers. She heard the woman say something next to her. Something about *it's been doing this lately* or something like that. But she didn't quite catch it all. The screen would flicker with a bluish colour every now and then, the voices behind her faded as if she was slowly drifting away from them and she tried to tune her ears into the white noise of the telly. She wanted so badly to try and make out what she thought she could hear just under the white noise. She hadn't blinked for quite a while, and when she suddenly tried to, it seemed that she couldn't. She thought she heard her name. But she couldn't have. But then she heard it again. And then suddenly,

"Evelyn!" shouted the Captain, right next to her ear.

The Captain had just seen Evie and Shemas' wife staring at the T.V. screen, heads cocked to one side and being drawn closer and closer to it.

He lunged over to it and switched it off.

"Hey, what did you do that for?" said Evie.

"Here, that's my telly."

"You mustn't watch the television," the Captain said. "From now on, this stays *off*, understand?"

"You can't tell me not to watch me own television."

"I'm sorry but it's for your own good," he said grabbing Evie's hand.

"You won't forget?" Shemas called to him.

"No I won't. Thank you Shemas." He was pulling Evie along with him as he was scooting out of the house. "And don't listen to your radio either!" He added.

"What do you mean? What's wrong with the T.V. and radio?" Shemas asked.

"No time to explain. But if you want to keep a grip on your own minds, then do as I say, please." He darted out through the doorway after he'd pushed Evie out, shut the door behind him and started down the street again.

"Why did you rush out of the house like that? You were supposed to find out where the broadcasting centre is."

"I did find out. That's what we were talking about the whole time."

"Who?"

"That man, Shemas and I."

Evie was astounded and she stopped on the road, "I didn't hear *any* of that."

The Captain stopped and walked back to her. "That's probably because you were so entranced by the television."

She was a little confused, "Well I couldn't stop watching it."

The two could feel tiny drops of water on their heads and arms, and they started to hear the pattering of rain on the rooftops nearby. Evie looked up and saw that clouds had gathered and soon it started to pour. She was flabbergasted by the sudden change of weather, but this was the least of her reasons to be flabbergasted.

The Captain said softly to her, "You see what type of force we're dealing with here. It's the Ogrimite. Up there on the Satellite. It's started already. He's started to broadcast his news to the world. Quite a lot of people will have been watching their tellies, but how many more now, now that it's raining, mmm?"

"Nothing else to do on a rainy day, but sit and watch the box all day," Evelyn said rather pensively. "But not everyone will be watching the same thing."

"There's only one station, remember? And you already know how easy it is to get drawn in."

Evie looked frightened. She thought the *danger* would be sword-fighting big hairy aliens with ten eyes, blowing up spaceships and zooming around in the air, dodging missiles. Not an invisible enemy attacking deviously through radio waves and T.V. ariels.

The rain was making puddles fast. The dirt road was turning into a creak of shallow sloshy mud. Evelyn rolled her jeans up to her calves, put the hood of her jacket over her head and continued following the Captain—wherever he was going.

They had been doing a good solid walk in the rain for at least another five minutes and Evie thought how good it would be if they could get a lift. They might have done, if there were cars driving around, but there weren't any. There were some along the side of the roads, parked, but none on the move. There was nobody in the streets walking about either. No signs of life, with the exception of Evelyn and the Captain.

"Where is everybody?" asked Evie.

"Home, out of the rain."

"What, are they scared of it or something?"

They were just passing another block of long, narrow houses.

"Possibly," the Captain replied. "Who knows?"

"Is your name really Captain Johns?"

"What? Oh. You really must try and stay on the topic at hand, Evelyn."

Just as she passed a curtain-less window, she saw a couple sitting in front of their television set.

"Captain, those people are watching T.V."

He stopped, faced Evie and joined her at the window. "Something needs to be done."

"We should tell them!"

The Captain spun around, walked to the couple's door and knocked.

When they answered, he boldly said, "Hello, I'm Captain Pauls and this is my friend Evelyn. Now, I'm sorry to inform you that you will be unable to watch your television for the rest of the afternoon, or, until further notice."

"What are you on about? It's working fine."

"Aren't you getting that flickering trouble, with the sort of, blue light?" Evie asked.

"Yeah, on and off, but we don't mind."

"Then I'm very sorry, but I'll have to fix it for you," said the Captain pushing his way into their home. He headed straight for the television, attended to the back of it and pulled out one of the wires getting himself a small electric shock.

"What do you think you're doing, coming in here . . ."

"I'm very sorry, but it's for your own good. Do *not* watch television . . ." he found a radio built into a wall above the T.V. screen and disconnected this too, ". . . *or* listen to the radio, alright? Tell your neighbours. Tell your friends!" He ran back out of the house to find Evie still on the doorstep.

She closed the door after him. "They didn't seem very convinced; I don't think they're going to tell their friends. And we don't have time to knock on every single door in the neighbourhood."

"Try the *world*."

"Well what are we going to do?"

"As soon as I get to that broadcasting centre, my plan is to broadcast over the top of the Ogrimite up there.

Only, I don't know how long it'll take me to accomplish that, so we'll have to split up."

"Split up? But, this is an alien planet, I don't know my way around."

"This is my first visit too, remember? All you have to do is continue telling people not to watch T.V. or listen to their radios."

". . . Or use their iStreams."

"Yes, although I understand that's quite a new and expensive gadget, not many people will have one yet. So, do you understand what to do?"

"Yes, but, how will we meet up again? We should have some form of communication. What if I get lost?"

"Um . . ." the Captain was patting all his pockets. He just *knew* he had something for the occasion, ". . . here, use this . . ."

"You have a phone? A mobile phone?" Evie was in awe and awfully excited. Her mum wasn't going to let her have a mobile phone until she turned sixteen. She suddenly thought of her mum♣ and how little she'd thought of her until now . . . and how much she suddenly missed her.

The Captain finally whipped out what he was looking for. It wasn't a mobile phone. It was a big, black, chunky, block of plastic with a wonky aerial sticking out of one end.

"How did *that* fit in your pocket?"

"With quite a lot of difficulty."

"And what use is one?"

"Oh don't worry, I've got another one." He whipped a second one out of the same pocket. "So, if anything's

♣   . . . who incidentally at this very moment was watching T.V. back on Earth.

the matter, press that button, and talk into it. But when you've finished talking, you have to release the . . ."

"I know how to use a walky-talky." She grabbed it from him.

"Well this is not just a walky-talky but ah . . . I'll show it off some other time. I'm going to find that broadcasting centre. If Shemas was correct, it should only be another three streets away."

"Okay," Evie said still looking at him.

"Okay," he said back.

"Right."

"Right. I'll be off then."

"Right."

"No *left. I* go right, you go left. And be careful."

"Right you are! . . . and left I am. See you soon." Evie was a little nervous about this task of hers. People didn't appreciate people just bursting into their homes and telling them not to watch their own tellies or listen to their own radios. But she knew the damage that this Ogrimite was already doing to people through their television sets—it had already almost happened to her. She was being brainwashed in seconds and the same would happen to these people in their homes on these very streets, only there wouldn't be a Captain standing close by to tear them away from it. It was Evie this time. Evie had to do the tearing away. She was the tearer-awayer.

She went left, came to a new street of houses and made a start.

The Ogrimite was blobbing here and there across all the turned-on equipment in the news room of the satellite. Every three seconds, he pumped a telepathic energy through the system, sending inaudible, invisible messages through to the world below. He looped the signals so they would repeat over and over again automatically, so that he could now do something else.

He concentrated very hard, (and you could tell because the glow of blue light within him swelled and dimmed and swelled and dimmed), and in no time at all, he had contact with a friend. And this friend, another Ogrimite, was situated in an Ogrimite spaceship hovering over a planet near by, waiting for an order to send eight hundred and fifty two more Ogrimites to the planet Serothia.

Chapter Eleven

A Miraculous Find

It was so intriguing, so inviting and so alluring; Lenny could not take her eyes off of it. She didn't know what was so interesting about it, but somehow the calming sound, the wavy picture and the gentle pulsing of a blue light was relaxing and it made her mind feel completely at rest. No need to think. No need to concentrate. No need to ponder or worry about anything. It was almost as if her mind was being run for her. That everything was under control, her life was under control, her thoughts were under control; her whole mind was under control. It was a good feeling. She had passing thoughts of things she had to get done around the house, but there was no way she could get up and do them while this fascinating feature was on the telly. She remembered she had left the clothes ironer going and it should have been beeping by now to tell her it was done, but she hadn't heard the beeping, so she left it. And soon, she forgot it. She soon wanted to let her mind forget everything. The oven, the video-phone, the letters she had to write, the bills, her job, friends' birthdays, her parents, *was that a knock at the door . . . no it couldn't have been, I didn't hear it.* Lenny tried to concentrate on the television. She thought she heard a girl's voice somewhere within the white noise, or maybe it was inside her head. Lenny couldn't tell. Then came the thumping. *Was this what really happened when you watch too much T.V.? You hear thumping noises in your head, almost feel the vibrations?* She really had no idea how long she had been sitting there for. She seemed to have lost all sense of the time. She might have been watching the telly for five minutes, or five hours—again, she couldn't tell. And the thumping got louder. Slow, crisp thumps along with that voice as well. That annoying voice that Lenny wished would just go away.

The next time Lenny thought about it, the noises *had* gone away, and there was a young girl scurrying around to the back of her house. Then Lenny went blind. And before she started panicking, she blinked a little and realised she could see a few things around the outside of her vision—around the outside of the television. Her eyes moved off the black screen and she got a fright when she suddenly saw a young girl standing by the television. "What did you do that for?" Lenny erupted. "And *what* do you think you're doing inside my house? I didn't invite you in! Get out now!"

"I'm sorry," the girl said, "but this was urgent, you were watching T.V."

"Yes, I was blooming well enjoying it, too." The young woman reached for her remote control.

The girl had the cheek to snatch it from her and unplug the T.V. altogether.

"What on Serothia do you think you're doing?!"

"It's dangerous, you can't watch T.V. Can't you understand you were being brainwashed?"

"Brainwashed? Ridiculous."

"What do you remember just then?"

"Well I was . . . watching that . . . thing on television . . . and then you came in."

"But didn't you hear me knocking? Didn't you hear me calling out?"

She shook her head slowly. "No, I . . . must have been so engaged in what was on the telly. Easy to do, only . . . come to think of it, I don't even seem to remember what I was watching. And *what* is that annoying beeping noise?"

"Never mind about that! It's just important that you don't use your television or your radio. Do you have an iStream?"

"I don't . . . think . . . I . . . do . . . What's an iStream? What's that beeping?"

"I don't know," Evie said getting frustrated. She looked around quickly and walked a little way down the hall. "It's this . . . thing, called a *Premium Clothes Ironer.*" Evie paused. *A machine to do your ironing?* "Cool."

"Clothes ironer? I don't have a clothes ironer . . . do I?"

After a while, Evie seemed to be able to convince the lady that she was being brainwashed and not to use the T.V. or radio. She told her to tell her friends and moved onto the next house in the road.

She dragged her feet, exhausted from *one* house. *This is going to take a long, long time*, she thought to herself, *and only about one per cent will ever believe me!*

It was still drizzling down. She started knocking, and when she put her ear to the door, she could hear the static from a television set blaring.

The Captain did not need to go much further to reach the broadcasting centre. After turning the last corner, he had realised, thankfully, that the place was impossible to miss. It was a large oddly shaped building—not your average four walls, multiple floors and roof. The whole thing was made up of irregular shapes that almost looked like they had just been stuck on here and there with glue and sticky tape. But the Captain had seen many buildings on many different planets, and so he had seen weirder.

He ran up to it and bolted through the double doors. Nothing much was happening inside; there were not many people about. But when he did see someone, they were clearly dazed and mesmerised by the vibrations that were pumping through the place. Everyone had forgotten their job, forgotten they existed. The Captain immediately covered his ears realising what was going on, and rushed past a few people and a set of offices in search of a pair of good head-phones.

He found some, and slapped them over his ears quickly, pleased by the amount of sound it cut out. He could tell they would do the trick because there wasn't really any sound in the place to begin with, but they still made the atmosphere considerably quieter. They would ensure that he was not going to be brainwashed by the great hypnotising Ogrimite.

People took no notice of him as he ran up all the flights of stairs to get to the top. He took the stairs in huge strides—two at a time. There was no time to lose. On the way, he noticed lots of monitors all showing what was broadcasting around the world. They all showed a flickering screen of static, occasionally giving off a blue light. He heard no sound of course, but he guessed it wouldn't have been much to listen to—just the sound of the static. But through the sound, he knew were subliminal messages saying, *Forget. Forget. Forget. Follow me. Follow me. We, the Ogrimites are your Lords and Masters. Obey me. Obey me.*

On the next landing he arrived at, he happened to look up at the monitor there, and it was blank. No picture at all—not even the static. He made sure it was turned on, fiddled with it a bit and found no fault. This, made him move even faster. It meant that the Ogrimite must have temporarily run out of power and now it would go back to get more. At least, no new people were going to be brainwashed for a while. But this small mercy came at the expense of lots and lots of people up on Satellite SB-17, who were now in danger of being absorbed.

"Did you hear that?" said Lisa to the others up on the Bridge of the Satellite.

"I don't know," James replied looking around cautiously.

Things had been quiet for quite a while. No worry from the Ogrimite that they could tell.

Paulo was making the way safe for another uninvited passenger on the Satellite. The system, without fail, was bringing another poor soul from Earth, thinking it was bringing another properly trained worker to help. The tube by the wall gleamed a white light and there in the space appeared a skinny young gentleman with a business suit and glasses. He stumbled out when Paulo opened the tube. Of course he was confused and disorientated, and Paulo had to explain the whole business to him, when suddenly, they all heard what Lisa thought she'd heard before.

Mmmrrrreeeeaaarrrrrgh.

"It's on the move again," said James.

The little girl clinging onto Lisa's leg started to squeal.

"What do we do?" Lisa said.

"We confuse it again. Move around lots. The others down below will hopefully realise the monster again and stop moving."

"But I was on my way to work," said the man in a foreign accent. "How long is this going to take?"

"I'm afraid none of us have a choice," Paulo said jogging around the Bridge.

"Well I refuse to participate."

"Fine. But give me your briefcase."

"Why on earth should I . . ."

"Just give it to me, please," Paulo said with authority.

The man obeyed him, (yet he felt very vexed at the thought of taking orders from a mere teenager).

Paulo grabbed it and started tossing it up in the air and catching it while jogging around the room. Lisa was dancing and flying around the room like a butterfly with the young girl, and James was star-jumping.

"Loopy!" the man said. "You're all loopy!"

Evie burst into another house where a young man was watching T.V.

"Turn off that T.V.!" she yelled, but then froze in front of it.

"What are you talking about, girl? Why should I? I'm only watching a repeat of *Car World*."

Evie was staring at the T.V. and she was perplexed. "You are too."

"Here, listen, why are you in my house?"

Evie looked at the gentleman for the first time and she noticed he was very good looking. When she started talking, she was furious at her body for suddenly doing all that automatic, nervous, flirtatious behaviour against her will. How silly it was when he was much older than her. He *looked* about thirty two, but on Serothia his age would have been fifty something.

"Did you hear me? Why are you in my house?"

"Oh, well . . . the T.V., your T.V. was dangerous."

"Dangerous?"

"Well before, when it was all snowy, it could have brainwashed you. And I'm not being silly, I'm being serious."

"Well I wasn't watching when it was snowy. I just turned it on."

Evie sighed heavily and gave a smile. "That's a relief . . . But I don't understand why it's normal now." She sat for a while watching *Car World* but thinking about the Ogrimite.

"Well . . . was . . . that it?" the man asked after what seemed like ages.

She snapped out of a daze. "Oh . . . yes, that was it, really."

"Well . . . do you mind . . ." he gestured toward the door.

"Oh, of course, I'll er . . . I'll just . . ." she got up and started heading for the door. Then she smiled and said, "My name's Evie," then she edged back into the room and put on a more serious tone, ". . . and I should probably stay. Because if that T.V. goes snowy again, well . . . I'll be here."

The man laughed. "My name's Rona, and I think I can look after myself."

"No, no, you don't understand." Suddenly, there were funny crackling noises coming from her pocket. She realised what it was and then grabbed it. "Captain?"

"The Ogrimite's stopped to get more energy and you know what that means. We need to move fast."

"Well it's a good thing for these people down here. But it's going to be hard to convince them that they're being brainwashed when it's not on. It was hard enough when it *was* on." She could feel Rona looking at her as if she was a nut. She smiled at him over her shoulder, then returned to the walky-talky. "What are *you* doing?"

His words were broken up and had a stress behind them, so Evie assumed he was working on something as he spoke. "I'm *wor*-king on *cut*ting *off* the *con*-tact between the Satellite and this broadcasting . . . *sta*-tion."

"Well you keep doing that and I'll keep trying to convince this man that his T.V. is . . ."

"No, you've got to get around to as many houses as possible. You've told him once, that's enough."

Does the Captain know *how handsome this guy is?* Evie thought.

"It doesn't matter how pretty the boys are," he said next, "just get moving! You're too young to be noticing that kind of thing anyway." Then he said, "Over and out."

Evie was embarrassed. This wasn't a mobile phone where whatever the person is saying on the other end can only be heard if your ear is right up to the speaker, this was a walky-talky . . . thing.

She turned around. He was smiling. It was a nice smile, but a patronising one. One that someone might display to a fourteen year old. "If that T.V. goes snowy again, just turn it off straight away! Better still, turn it off now! Otherwise you'll be brainwashed by an Ogrimite, okay? And don't use the radio!" She was heading for the door again. "Just please trust me. Do you have an iStream?"

He shook his head.

"Well . . . good. Trust me, do as I say, and . . . you'll be . . . not brainwashed. Goodbye." She left quickly and headed around the corner to the next house.

But Rona's house was the last of a big group of houses. The next thing she came to was a much larger building surrounded by a tall fence. Her eyes scanned over it. It looked a bit like a school. Multiple long one-story buildings, one two-story building over to one side, and a big courtyard in the centre. She decided to run up to it to try and work out what it was. There were possibly lots of T.V.s in there that should be turned off. She reflected on her thinking, and she felt as if she was a rampaging mother obsessed with people reading books and being active rather than watching T.V. *All T.V.s everywhere must be turned off! I'm going to change the world by turning Serothia's T.V.s off!* Then it suddenly hit her. In this brief moment of jest she'd come to realise, she was *saving* the world . . . Well, a little piece of it, anyway. She didn't think she was doing a very good job of it so far, but that's what she was trying to do. This wasn't even *her* world and she was desperately trying to stop its people getting brainwashed and brought under the control of the Ogrimite. But people didn't listen to her. They thought she was a fool! They thought she was mad! Her words were folly to most of the people in the homes she visited. But Evie knew that this was life and death! Why couldn't they understand that? How could she get through to them? Out of all the homes she'd been in so

131

far, she had not worked out the answer. But what was this place in front of her? She felt that she *should* go and see. Something was telling her to approach.

She stood at a gate in the fence, and soon a man approached with an interesting type of uniform on. He was short, tough looking, and had stubble on his face.

"Yeah?" he asked.

"Excuse me, what is this place?"

"You from another village or something?"

"Yes. Yes, definitely."

"It's called the Satellite base. Where people are trained up to go and work on the Satellite up there."

Evie's mouth dropped open. No wonder she was drawn to this place.

"Why? You wanna be a recruit?"

Evie was frozen in position. The man was looking at a thirty-year-old little girl with her mouth wide open.

"Hello? You right?"

She shook her head and whispered, "I can't believe it. I can't believe it."

"Do you mind saying what you want? I got a busy day."

Suddenly, Evie was back. "The Satellite. It's in trouble!"

"What?"

"Satellite SB-17 yeah? It's in trouble, *Paulo's* in trouble. He needs new workers desperately, only the thingy-ma-gig isn't working."

". . . The transmat system?"

"Yeah, that thing! It's all gone wrong. You need to send workers up there to fix it!"

"But how? The thingy-ma-gig's not working, you just finished telling me."

"I don't know but . . . wait." She got out her walky-talky. "Captain, come in, Captain!"

It was a short while until he answered. "What is it," he said, sounding quite relaxed.

"I've found the place!"

"Place. Could you try to be more specific please?"

"The *thing* . . . place, you know . . ."

"Satellite base," said the short man.

"Satellite base!" Evie said. "Where workers are trained to work on Satellite SB-17."

"How did you come by that?" The Captain was excited now.

"I just, sort of, turned a corner and there it was!"

"Wait there, and I'll join you. Just as soon as I've *fixed* this . . . *what*-sa-ma-*call*-it . . . *do*-flacky." He added quickly, "Try and find someone who'll be best suited for the job of fixing the Satellite's transmat system before I get there."

"Righto! Over and out." She smiled. She'd always wanted to say that for real. "Well, are you gunna let me in?" she asked the man.

"Well er . . . I don't know. You see, you're not actually authorised."

"Oh, come on, I've proved that I know about the Satellite. And *Paulo*, I know Paulo! Can't you contact the Satellite, he'll vouch for me."

"There's been no communication from the Satellite in months. We've tried fixing it from here but we think the problem lies up there."

"Well you'll just have to trust me. Please, this concerns the future of this planet, and a whole lot of people from Earth as well!"

"Very well. But I'll be keeping a watch on you." He opened the locks on the gate. "And you'll have to wear this. All visitors must wear them at all times. It'll help us keep an eye on you and make sure you don't go anywhere you shouldn't be." He fastened a wrist band on her.

"Why, what have you got to hide?" She walked through into the courtyard.

"Nothing, but trainees ought not to be distracted.

Evie seemed to accept this as he led her inside.

"I noticed you said *Captain*. The person you communicated with on that device. What kind of Captain is he?"

"I don't really know. He's the Captain of a train I guess. And he's kind of my . . . acquaintance. That's all." She paused, and the man didn't say anything more. "He said I'm to find a worker who's best trained to fix the Satellite's transmat system. Is there anyone here who's qualified for that yet?"

"I'll take you to the maintenance section."

"But Paulo's a maintenance worker, and he said he didn't know how to do it. He needs someone who knows how to operate it."

"Perhaps Paulo was too young and too inexperienced to start work." The man paused for a short moment and blinked. "I will take you somewhere where you will be of much better use."

"What? No, I just need to find a worker."

"All that will be done, Evelyn, in good time. But first you must come with me, this way."

"Why?"

"A mere formality for visitors. A mundane procedure, but it must be undertaken."

He was walking quite briskly with such wide strides. He suddenly seemed to be in a hurry. He had taken Evie by the hand and was pulling her along and she had trouble trying to get her legs to move quickly enough. And all this time, while he was taking her across the courtyard to do this mundane task, she was racking her brain, trying to remember when she had told him her name.

Chapter Twelve

The Grim Neeper

The last do-flacky was disconnected from the thingy-ma-bob and the Captain was just about ready to step into the news room and connect himself up to a microphone.

"No more messages from Mr Ogrimite today, thank you," the Captain said, and he plugged in a few thick leads here and there, flicked on a few switches and wheeled a big camera over from the corner of the room to a position in front of a clearly set up news desk. He turned it on, raked his fingers through his dark brown, wavy hair and then prodded at a few strands in the front. He walked over to the desk, ran his tongue across both rows of his teeth and sat down.

"So, what's your name anyway?" Evie said as she was being led into a stuffy linoleum corridor. Very like school. The man in front of her, now pulling her by the wrist, was walking with such purpose and direction, that he paid no attention to his companion's question.

Evie was beginning to feel frightened, but she dare not show it, for fear of looking guilty of something. Plus, she didn't know if she had any reason to be frightened at all. And she had had instances where she'd worked herself up into a terrified stupor and then felt ridiculous for it afterwards.

The man had changed though. That was definite. He was different from when she had first met him. It seemed to be soon after she had mentioned the Captain. He wasn't as friendly now—not that he was overly friendly before. But she'd mentioned the Captain and that he was an acquaintance, and suddenly he'd acted differently. This caused Evie to keep coming back to the horrible feeling that this man was an enemy of the Captain, and therefore, an enemy of her's. But then, an even worse thought came to her. How long had she known the Captain? A day? It felt a lot longer, but it definitely was only a day or less. Maybe *he* was the enemy.

She struck down the thought straight away, but it kept creeping back slowly like a giant blue blob searching out its prey.

All of a sudden, she bumped into the man and immediately realised he'd stopped at a closed door. The door required his key-card and apparently, this was no issue. He simply took one from around his neck and swiped it in the lock. The door slid open.

Before them both was a very dark room. There were windows, but they had been covered over from the outside with large sheets of black material. The man was hiding his motives for dragging her to this place no more. He shoved her inside and said plainly, "Your acquaintance, the Captain is arriving here soon . . ."

Evie opened her mouth to respond *yes*, but it had not been a question put to her.

". . . and so it is important he does not find you."

"Why?" Evie was suddenly struck with fear. Why had she followed this man so willingly? She at least could have put up a bit of a fight. "Why is it important that he does not find me?"

"Because he must not succeed. And you must not interfere." He spoke almost robotically. "I must follow the leader."

Evie was about to try and make a run for it, but just as she flinched into movement, the door was slammed shut, leaving her in total disquieting darkness.

There were a lot of mindless people wandering around the Satellite SB-17 training grounds. The Ogrimite was in their heads, and they were blank slates on which the Ogrimite could start sketching. But they were like an army with no orders. Troops with no Commander. The Ogrimite had wiped their brains clean and then gone off to get more energy. They were stranded in a strange place they did not recognise, not knowing their own names.

Only Stretch so far had had orders. And that was to get the girl out of the way, and kill this Captain when he got here. Then, the Orgimite and its fellow comrades could come and take over the world. Stretch had locked Evelyn in the dark room, and was now heading for the main entrance again. The Captain was sure to show up soon.

On his way out, someone bumped into him on their way through one of the corridors.

"Stretch!" he said. This younger man was very tall and lean, had dark hair and was wearing orange, full-sleeve training overalls. "I've been looking for you. The boss wants a chat. Hey, have you seen the T.V. lately?"

"Yes," he simply answered.

"I mean like, in the last minute or so. There's some guy on there I've never seen before. He's talking rubbish about some hostile alien who wants to brainwash us all through the telly, and he's saying not to watch it. Or use the radio or anything else that gets broadcasts from the satellite. If you ask me, he's pretty daft. He's saying all this stuff as if it's important, but he's using T.V. to say it. How do we know *he's* not the hostile alien ey? Or, if he's not and he's trying to save us, if we all do what he says and turn off all the T.V.s, we won't hear the rest of what he's got to say."

Stretch stood there for a moment, looking up at him. Then, very blandly, he said, "There are no such things as aliens."

"Well I don't really believe there is either, but you never know. I'm open-minded. Although technically, there *is* such thing as aliens because it's another word for foreigners isn't it. If someone from Heywynn came over here to Ploth, they'd be an alien wouldn't they." He turned away from Stretch and pointed down the corridor from where he had come. "Even if a non-satellite worker person came in here and they knew nothing about anything, you know, about working on the satellite, then *they'd* be referred to as an alien." He turned back to Stretch, "*And* scientists, right? When they find a foreign fibre in . . ."

Stretch was gone.

"Stretch?" He said timidly. He was nicknamed 'Stretch' because of a friendly sarcastic joke on his height—or lack of. "Stretch?" He called out this time. "That's just rude." He was confused at his friend and colleague's behaviour. He frowned to himself, knowing that it wasn't usual for him to be so rude like that. He had had other people sometimes wandering off while he was speaking. He'd never been able to work out why, but Stretch—he never did. He was a friendly one. He always listened.

He shrugged, tried to forget it, and headed back to where he had come from.

It was the lunch room where he now came to. A few people were still in there on a break watching the last couple of minutes of this new guy's news flash.

*Please don't ignore me. I know how preposterous all this sounds, but you must **not** watch anymore television, listen to anymore radio or use your iStreams . . .*

"Ha," one bloke said, "I wish."

Don't take this lightly. It concerns the control of your own mind as I've already said. It concerns your lives, and the life of Serothia! Read a book. Have a sleep. Go for a run. Anything, but watch television, use the radio or an iStream. So as soon as I go off which will be in a second, TURN YOUR T.V. OFF! Thank you.

The screen flickered, and then displayed a few characters squabbling on a film set—half way though a comedy program.

"Well, that was weird," one guy said from a chair right in front of the television.

"Aren't you going to do what he said?"

"What? Turn the set off? You gotta be joking Squirt. Not right in the middle of my favourite program."

Squirt, the one who had been talking with Stretch, strode over and turned the television off. Then he unplugged it.

There were loud jeers, boos and hisses from the room. Someone even threw their unfinished sandwich at him.

"Well you never know! What harm could it do us? We've got some work to do anyway. Well I know I have. And I'm not going to get brainwashed by a hostile alien!"

He strode out of there, with his head high. He was a shy type, but he knew how to stand up for things he believed in and look after himself. He was nicknamed Squirt because he was the youngest trainee there at the moment. Being so very tall added the joke element to his nickname too, and when Squirt befriended the shorter man, (whose actual name was Marak Neeper) everybody decided to call *him* Stretch. But although he was the youngest, he was very gifted at many things, very intelligent and skilled at what he was training for. For this, however, he was occasionally hassled. Stretch had been the only one who didn't jeer at him in joke.

One of the men came up to him just as he was passing through the door. It was the one who'd been sitting right in front of the screen. He grabbed his arm. "Look, there's no harm in watching a bit of telly. I didn't see anyone being brainwashed in that room, did you? Now, go and put it back on, *Squirt.*"

Squirt yanked his arm out of the man's grasp. "If you want it on, you can put it on yourself, I won't be responsible." He then spoke quieter. "I don't know if you've noticed, but there are people in this place who aren't acting their usual selves. Even Stretch is acting strangely. I reckon he's been brainwashed."

"Yeah right."

"You go and find someone who looks . . . strange, empty. You go and ask them their name, where they live, what this place is. I don't reckon they'd be able to tell you."

The man hesitated for a short moment, but then he doubted. "Get out of town. There's no aliens. There's no brainwashing going on. It's all just some stupid hoax."

Stretch knocked on the door marked "BOSS".♣

There was a faint "Come in," from inside, and so he turned the door knob and slowly drifted in.

"Ah, Neeper," he addressed him by his real name. "Thanks for coming so quickly. Tell me, has there been any communication from Satellite SB-17 since the last time I enquired?"

"No," he replied truthfully.

"Nothing at all? Not even an attempt?"

"No."

"That's very unusual. And now there's this issue with the broadcasting."

"Someone is telling the world not to watch television."

"Are you feeling alright, today, Marak? You seem a little . . . flat."

"Yes."

"Probably some hoax to stir things up. We've had them before."

"Undoubtedly."

"Except I can't get passed the fact that no one's contacted from the Satellite. And the fact that someone's been able to broadcast their own message. There's obviously been a breach of security over at the centre."

♣ The position's official title had been changed so many times over the decades of the establishment's operation, that there ended up being a three metre long name-plate pinned to the outside of the door. It was stolen in a major burglary one night for the silver that it was plated with, and because of an 'in-joke' that developed amongst the employees, the simple word "BOSS" was written on the door in black texta. It remains there like that today.

"Yes."

"Well that's not my job. That's for the boss over there to deal with. Why aren't you saying 'yes, *Sir*'?"

"No reason . . . Sir."

"We'll have to send some people up to the Satellite I think. Just a . . . technician and an operator I think. They'll fix whatever's wrong up there."

Marak Neeper stood there, said and did nothing.

"Well, what are you waiting for? Organise this at once. Pick two well-trained workers and send them up there as soon as possible!"

Nothing.

The boss stood up out of his chair. "If you don't follow orders, I'll suspend you."

Still, nothing.

". . . Fire you?"

No response. Except for a slightly malevolent stare.

The boss started to walk around to the front of his desk. "I'll have to do it myself. If anyone's in trouble up there, we're their rescue!"

Stretch had had his hands behind his back, and now he slowly brought his right hand around to the front, revealing to the boss what he had been holding. He was clutching a small triangular gun and aiming straight at the helpless man. Before he could say another word, before he even had a chance to cry for help or even show some surprise, the trigger was pulled.

The T.V. was up loud. Others in the building were busy working. The shot was not heard by anyone.

Chapter Thirteen

The Captain Arrives

The task at the Broadcasting Centre had been a lot easier than the Captain had imagined. He had managed to broadcast a message all around the globe from a news room right under their noses. Authorities at the centre still had no idea what had gone on. While this was a good thing and something to be thankful for, the Captain knew that it meant that most, if not, all of the workers at the centre had been near a T.V. monitor or listening to the radio before he arrived. He had seen the televisions on when he arrived, the blue flickering, snowy screen, and he'd feared the worst. No one cared that he was there using all their equipment, because they probably had no clue where they were or what planet they were on.

Now, however, the Captain was standing outside the gates of a training complex. He had not been able to get through to Evie again to ask directions, but he knew it can't have been far away since Evie found it so quickly. He simply asked a lonely soul who'd been strolling along the street *not* watching television. After the kind man had obliged in giving him directions, the Captain had stressed to him what he'd just broadcasted on T.V.

"Hello," said the Captain to a man standing at the gate.

"Good day," the man replied tipping his head slightly.

The rain had died down and left little puddles of mud here and there. There was one right at the entrance of the gate, but the Captain showed no concern for it. Stretch, standing inside the training grounds could see that this man was in a hurry. He had a look of determination in his face—purpose, anxiousness to get inside. Unmistakeably, this man was the Captain.

"A friend of mine, Evelyn Bamford came here not long ago. She probably introduced herself as Evie." He was talking to a blank, expressionless face. "She's expecting me, I need to catch up with her." There wasn't any response, so the Captain kept on talking. "She must have mentioned me. This is urgent, I need to get inside. This is a matter of life and death—lots of deaths if I don't do something. There are people on Satellite SB-17 who are in trouble, and Evelyn should have been picking some of the best trained workers to go up there and help!"

It was a short while until Stretch spoke. "There's been no girl here. And if you don't mind me saying, it sounds like you've gone potty, sir."

"Ah-ha! How did you know my friend was a *girl*? Through the ages, Evelyn has been known to be both a male *and* female name." Liars had made this mistake so often.

"You said *she*, sir."

The Captain's shoulders noticeably sunk. He knew somehow, though, that this man was lying. And he could just guess why. The man didn't have the same mindless stare as the others he'd seen roaming about who had been brainwashed by the Ogrimite, but he guessed that this was because he had been given a purpose. He'd been given a job, and that was to stop anyone from hindering the Orgimite's mission up on the Satellite. Ogrimites were an incredible creature. Although they had no sense of hearing or sight as a human hears and sees, its other senses, touch and vibration awareness were exceptional. They also had an ability to feel with the mind—what some people might call intuition; and their telepathic abilities were also difficult to comprehend. The fact that the man in front of him had been brainwashed by the broadcast and was now being controlled by the Ogrimite became clear to the Captain when he'd tried once more to get inside the gate by saying, "I can save the lives of everyone on this planet if you let me pass!", and the man had replied, "Alright, you can enter."

He'd said it very blandly, and the Captain knew that it wasn't what he'd just said that made the man let him in, but a much greater influence. Once under an Ogrimite's 'thumb', it can very easily communicate with you telepathically. And this is precisely what had occurred. While the Captain said "I can save the lives of everyone on this planet", the Ogrimite had said to him, "Let him in, and kill him. Otherwise, he'll roam free, and invent an alternative plot to stop the Ogrimites."

"Well, thank you very much," said the Captain, "how kind. Remind me to give you a tip, when I've got the change."

Stretch escorted the Captain towards the buildings and although he kept a firm grip on him, the Captain kept a sharp eye out for Evelyn.

Squirt was determined to get back to work, put his head down, ignore the others around him and just do what he knew was right. But on his way back to his training room, he happened to pass the fuse box on the wall. His eyes glued to it and he stopped in his tracks. He stood there for a moment biting his bottom lip. *I could turn off every telly in this place just with one flip of a lever.* He breathed deeply in and out, and then thought to himself with more courage, *I can't let them watch T.V. when it could be dangerous. I'm doing them a favour! They'll thank me afterwards!* So he opened the door of the box, and tugged on the lever, which was a little stiff. He was a fair way away from the lunch room by now, he didn't hear any groans of annoyance, but he trusted that it had worked. He replaced the door and left the vicinity.

The Captain was walked through some corridors, wondering where he was being taken. He started to make conversation, however it had a double purpose. "A lot of rooms you've got here. All training rooms are they? A different room for every different type of work." He was speaking quite loudly, although Stretch didn't respond to any of it. "Looks like a well-run establishment, nice and clean. Not much noise around. You wouldn't be able to use these rooms as secret prison cells would you," he made a little light-hearted laugh, "I mean, such thin walls, you'd be able to hear the person *cry for help*. Pretty useless. If anyone was here locked up, *I'd be able to hear them*; the *Captain*, that is. That's me, the Captain."

"We don't use them to lock people up," Stretch lied.

"Just as well, because it'd be pretty futile if you did. (Not very nice either, come to think of it.) Yes. Quite futile. Too many people roaming the corridors would hear them *calling out for help*." He felt doubtful. The man escorting him was sure to know what he was up to, and he was bound to be much cleverer than to just lock Evelyn in one of these rooms.

The Captain's head suddenly snapped up while they were passing numerous doors, as he thought he heard a distant cry. One little wail, a call for help. Evelyn?

There it was again. A voice—he was sure it was a voice, calling. His pace had slowed in reaction, trying to listen, but Stretch tugged at him to keep walking.

"Hey, hey, what's up with the brutality? Since when was I a prisoner?" asked the Captain with innocent eyes.

"Since now," said Stretch holding his odd-shaped gun against the Captain's side.

In reflex, the Captain raised his arms above his head, but his face showed anything but fear. He had a feeling things would go this way.

"Just keep moving," said Stretch, and the Captain complied with no argument.

Suddenly, Stretch stopped, and the Captain had to stop himself from having a joke with him by keeping on moving like he'd said, up the corridor. But he contained himself.

The televisions have been turned off where you are, said the Ogrimite in Stretch's head, *they must be turned on. More of your trained workmen will be useful for me. There must be no one there who is capable of being sent here to the Satellite to stop my plans.*

Stretch opened the nearest door, checked no one was in there, thrust the Captain inside and locked him in. Then he headed to the nearest intercom controls, which would relay his voice across the entire complex. He switched it on and spoke into it. "Attention all trainers and trainees. I announce a break for everyone. It's been reported that you have all been working very well and so the boss wants everyone, that's *everyone*, to take an indefinite break. Please, however, do not leave the complex." He paused, thinking. "You are all still on call and we may need you at anytime, but please relax in the lunch rooms, have a snack, put your feet up, and watch some telly."

Stretch then marched straight over to check the fuse box to see if there was any trouble there. He found the trouble, and rectified it. The lever was flipped, and the T.V.s came back on, everywhere.

"Great," the Captain pouted to himself, now that he was locked in a room himself. He thought coming to this place would solve all his problems. They'd find a capable worker, send him up to the Satellite, and the battle would be half over. But this place was nothing but corrupt. Their only hope against the enemy, and they'd all been brainwashed by it.

"What's great?" came a voice from within the room. "Has something good happened?"

The Captain turned around, startled, but he saw nobody. It was an utterly and completely person-less room—except for the Captain of course . . . and the guy crouching down behind the work bench.

The Captain saw a dark haired head first, then a forehead, then a pair of eyes, and then suddenly, the whole body popped up. A young man in orange overalls.

"You're the guy on T.V.!" he said, wide-eyed.

"Oh, you saw that. That's encouraging."

"Gee, I wish you could meet celebrities this easily *all* the time."

"I . . . I'm not a celebrity."

"Oh but you were very good. I did what you said. I turned the telly off straight after your little talk. You were so convincing."

For a moment, one could almost describe the Captain's cheeks as 'blushing'. He nearly got sidetracked. "Oh, well, thanks but er . . . but never mind that!" He remembered his urgency of saving the world. "Listen, what are you doing here?"

"This is where I train, where I practise my trade," he said. "What are *you* doing here?"

"I was tossed in here by . . . a man, short, nearly bald. Why were you hiding?"

"Hiding? Oh, I wasn't hiding, I was working on this piece of equipment down here, trying to fix it. I'm a technician. Well, training to be a technician. Although, I guess I sort of am one, because I've completed my apprenticeship more or less. I'm just working here and improving my skills until I get called up to work on the Satellite. That's what we're all here for. The people in this place anyway, not everyone in the whole world. I don't know exactly what we're *here* for, as in *on this planet*. That's quite a deep philosophical question, which people can spend hours debating, as I have, but I still haven't found an answer. But as far as this training place goes . . ."

"Right, right, I get it, I get it, but . . . where is everyone else? It looks like this room is meant to have a lot more than one person working in it."

"There usually is, but they're not here at the moment. Probably all slacking off. Where are you from anyway? I mean, why are you here? I don't mean, why are you here as in, the purpose of your life, I mean, why are you here, in this place to get tossed into a room by Stretch, or at least I think that's who it probably was that you described."

"The reason I'm here and the purpose of my life is much the same thing. I'm here to save the world. To save Serothia from being taken over by a scheming, deadly race of creatures called the Ogrimites."

Squirt stared at him. "Blimey. Don't know what you're going to do from inside a stuffy little room."

"I'm *locked in*. That man Stretch locked me in, and I believe that he's locked my friend Evelyn in a room somewhere as well."

"Why would he do that?"

"Because he's trying to stop me from saving the world."

"Why would he do that?"

"Because he's been brainwashed by the Ogrimite."

"Oh! That business you were talking about on the T.V.?"

"Yes!"

"I did what you said. Turned it off straight away I did. Didn't want to risk it, in case it was true."

"Well it is true, and I'm trapped in here unable to do anything."

"Oh it's alright. I switched all the tellies off from the main power."

"That's only a temporary solution. People all over the globe will be watching T.V.!"

Squirt saw the dilemma. "And listening to the radio. And all the richer people will no doubt be using their iStreams."

The Captain was nodding expectantly. Squirt was shaking his head and staring at the floor. "Well I don't know what you're going to do about that. Sorry, got no ideas."

"Well I actually have an idea, and I could succeed if I wasn't locked in this room." The Captain felt like he was going around in circles with this character.

"You're not locked in here," he said.

"What?"

"Well, if you want to get out, that's the easy part. I just can't imagine how you're going to stop the whole world from getting brainwashed by this Oggymite thing."

"You can get me out of here?"

"'Course I can. If he's locked that door, I can get it open again."

"How?"

"Every trainer and trainee here have a set of keys, which open most doors."

"*Most* doors?"

"Well, all except the boss's drawers and the safe and that. Fancy Stretch locking you in here. He must have had a good reason. Although I did notice he wasn't acting normal earlier. You think he's been brainwashed by that . . . that . . ."

"Ogrimite, yes, could you just . . ." he indicated towards the door.

"This could be serious then. I mean, if *anyone* can be brainwashed, that means . . . that means anybody could be brainwashed and we wouldn't know who! I mean, except for the subtle clues from their behaviour. None of the lads in the lunch room will get brainwashed, because I turned the T.V.s in this place off . . ."

"Yes, as you said before."

"As I said before. I mean, I'm still not sure if I believe all this is . . ."

"Look, I hate to be rude, but I'm rather eager to get out of this room and . . . you know, save the world."

"Oh, yeah, of course, sorry." He pulled out a small bundle of keys from underneath his overalls. They were hanging around his neck and he spent the next few seconds picking out the right one. "This one should do the trick." He walked over to the door and then said, half to the Captain and half to himself, "Ha, you can tell we don't usually use this place for locking people up, Stretch didn't do a very good job of it. He certainly wasn't expecting me to be in this room, anyway."

"Either that, or the brainwashing of the Ogrimite could very well have wiped some logic and thinking processes from his mind."

"Really?" He looked worried and concerned for his colleague as he opened the door up wide. "Will Stretch be okay . . . after all this, will there be permanent damage?"

"I can't say, I'm sorry. It's impossible to tell without examining him properly. Friend of yours?"

"Well, not really *friend*, more . . . well . . . yeah. He kind of is my friend, come to think of it, yeah. He's the only one here I ever really got along with. He's the only one that ever seemed to listen to me, because you see, you probably don't know this but, I have a tendency to talk a bit too much. You know, sometimes I can go on and on and on and never stop, and he listens. But he also lets me know when I'm raving on a bit too much as well, and that helps. You see, without that, I wouldn't know, I guess."

He could have gone on, but the Captain jumped in. "I will do everything I possibly can to help your friend return to his usual self."

Squirt didn't know why, but he believed him.

The Captain snapped into action suddenly and started heading off down the corridor.

"Here," said Squirt quickly, "who are you?"

"I'm the Captain." He stopped and paid him some attention. "I didn't catch your name."

"Around here, I'm known as Squirt. But my real name's Haron. I like Squirt though, I guess. Just grown used to it."

"You said you'd finished your training?"

"Yeah."

"And you're waiting to be called up to work on the Satellite?"

"Yeah."

"You might be just who we need. Come with me." Although he was a little exasperating, the Captain had taken a liking to Squirt. He was young, eager, enthusiastic, positive, and he believed the Captain when he said *this planet's in trouble.*

Squirt showed an excited expression, he closed the training room door behind him and followed the Captain instantly. And the two of them ran along the corridor. First job—rescue Evelyn. Second job—get Squirt up onto the Satellite.

Chapter Fourteen

Escape

Had I imagined it? Had I been hearing things? No. It's not possible, I did hear a voice. It was so clear; I just know it was the Captain! He's here. And he's not going to forget me. And he's certainly not one of the bad guys. He can't be. Unless this was all in his plan—to get me locked up and out of the way. He didn't want me with him on the Train, but I came anyway. And then he wanted me to stay on the Satellite, where that dangerous creature is! But I stowed away. Then he sent me on that horrible task of telling everyone not to watch T.V. while he went off and . . . All this time, he's been trying to get rid of me!

In the dark, there was nothing else for Evie to do, but think. She was working herself up more and more into a panic, giving herself reason to be afraid—and afraid of the Captain. The more she thought about it, the more she realised she shouldn't be trusting the Captain. She'd trusted him with so much already. Her life for one thing, the lives of her brother and friend, and now, for some reason, she was trusting he'd come back and rescue her from this grim, pitch black prison. However, the more she thought about this, the more hope she lost that anyone would come and get her out. Why should they?

She was finally out of the Captain's and anybody else's way. She would stay here for eternity. Alone, forgotten, hungry, thirsty, alone.

She tried banging on what she guessed was the door and calling out for help. But for all she knew, everyone in this place was her enemy. There could be ten people all on the other side of that door just standing there listening, and sniggering. Because there was no reply. No answer to her call. No glimmer of hope whatsoever.

The Captain and Squirt were running down yet another corridor—the Captain calling out Evie's name now and again, but receiving no reply.

Squirt got a terrible feeling there was something wrong. "This isn't right," he told the Captain.

"What? What's not right?"

"There's no one about, anywhere. I mean, usually, there's *someone* you bump into along these corridors. Usually lots of people."

"You said they could be on break?"

"Yeah *my* chaps; the one's who train in the same room as me, but not everybody at once, that's just ridiculous."

The Captain was still looking at Squirt, waiting for him to finish. Until, with delight, he realised that he *had* finished, and then he replied. "I suspect the work of the Ogrimite is here. We know that your friend Stretch at least has been affected. There could very well be more, and or, Stretch is trying to set up the place so that there *is* more. But at the moment, I'm glad there's no one to bump into in these halls, because it means that we won't have any trouble getting anywhere."

Squirt nodded his understanding of the Captain's stance.

"Now, you know this place well. Where might Stretch or anyone else have put Evelyn, to lock her up, get her out of the way?"

He shrugged, "Well, any one of these rooms I suppose."

"So, we have to check them all, get your keys out again."

"But then again, all these are in frequent use. You'd think that he'd put her in one that's not in use anymore."

"Are there any?"

"Yes, a few."

"Take me to them, then."

"Yes, sir." He gave a little salute with a smile and raced ahead of him, leading the way.

"Evelyn, I can manage on my own. You'll be safer here. And that's not a suggestion, that's an order . . . Evelyn, I told you to stay on the Satellite to look after your brother and everyone else . . . We'll have to split up. All you have to do is continue telling people not to watch T.V. or listen to their radios."

The Captain's words were whirring through Evie's mind. *It's true*, she thought, *I've lumbered him with my presence. He never wanted me with him. He's trying to get rid of me! Well he's done it, hasn't he? He's rid of me. I'm stranded here on an alien planet. Light-years away from home. My brother's in terrible danger and I can't do anything. I'm just sitting here waiting for the unthinkable to happen. I'll end up as a mindless, brainwashed, Ogrimite-obeying Serothian! Or just stay in here 'till I die, utterly and completely ALONE!*

Next thing, she thought she heard a voice.

Maybe not.

Yes! It was a voice. And it was calling out, what sounded like *Evelyn!*

"Evelyn?" called the Captain for the eleventh time.

"Most of these are still in use, but the two near the end down there, the old common room and the dark room, we've got new, bigger ones now, so naturally they're not used. Just junk rooms really."

"Evelyn?"

Evie got up onto her feet and pounded on the door. "Yes! Yes, in here!" All thoughts of the Captain being an enemy left her. Not because he now appeared to be rescuing her, but because she now had something else to do other than think. Trusting the Captain was sort of the default setting in Evie's mind.

"Was that her voice?" Squirt asked.

"It was *a* voice, Squirt. What, is there likely to be multiple people locked up in these rooms?"

"No . . . what? . . . I don't get it."

"Never mind," the Captain said feeling a bit regretful about his sarcastic snap at the boy. "Evelyn, call out again, we need to figure out where you are."

"Captain? I'm in here." She banged on the door again.

Immediately, the Captain knew where to go. "It's this room," he told Squirt. He spoke to Evie calmly through the door. "Don't worry, Evelyn, we've got some keys, we'll get you out."

"Ah . . . um . . ." said Squirt.

"Ah um? What do you mean ah um?" said the Captain.

"Well these old rooms were in use before they had the locks changed. There was a burglary around the same time as they were building the new common room and dark room and a bunch of others. We changed all the locks, didn't bother with these since they weren't going to be used anymore."

"Ah . . . um . . ." said the Captain. He tried to get over his fury quickly, without wasting time. "Okay, have a look round, what can we use?"

"I'm pretty good with a hair pin."

"Excellent! Well, off you go."

"Ah . . . um . . . haven't got a hair pin."

The Captain did a full turn and raked his fingers through his hair. "I've got some tools, only they're in the Train," he muttered under his breath.

"Captain, what's going on?" Evie said.

"It's alright, we're er . . . in the process. Any other ideas?" he asked Squirt.

"Without destroying training grounds property, not off the top of my head, no."

"Shhh," said the Captain.

"What?"

"Footsteps."

Squirt paused, then said, "Stretch's footsteps, I'd know them anywhere."

"He has a gun."

"A gun?" Squirt exclaimed.

"Shhh." The Captain spoke in a raspy whisper. "A sort of triangle, metal thing, with a handle and trigger poking out at the bottom. Small, bluey, grey-y."

"Oh, one of those! They're for emergencies."

"We've got to get out of here. Quick." The Captain was looking around on the walls, and the walls of the hallway just around the corner. And around the corner, he saw something that was pleasing to the eye.

"But how?" asked Squirt in a high-pitched whisper.

The Captain, breaking a glass cabinet mounted on the wall and grabbing the axe from inside said, "You gave me the idea when you said *damaging training grounds property*. Thanks very much!" And he raised the axe in the air, shouted, "Evie, get away from the door!" and slammed it down into the wood with all his strength.

"You're damaging training grounds property!" said Squirt, still whispering. "And you're making too much noise, Stretch will definitely know we're here now!"

"Desperate times, call for desperate measures." He swung again at the door. He could see Evie cowering in the corner, shielding her face from flying splinters of wood. He took one last swing at the door with the axe, just as Stretch appeared from around the corner up at the far end of the corridor.

"Can you fit through there, Evelyn?"

She got up and ran towards the hole in the door.

"Duck!!" Squirt yelped, as he saw Stretch raise up the arm with which he was holding the gun.

They ducked and so did Evie. The Captain held out his hand through the hole and Evie took it firmly.

Stretch had adjusted his aim down towards the two men crouching on the floor.

"What's the opposite of 'duck'?" Squirt shouted.

"I don't know, why?" the Captain shouted back.

Evie was climbing through the hole, and just spotted the gun aimed at the Captain and his companion. "I think the word 'run' will do!!"

"Right you are, come along!"

Stretch shot the gun again, and it hit the empty space on the floor where Squirt and the Captain were milliseconds before.

There were three running figures just disappearing around the corner.

"Is that a gun?" Evie shouted breathlessly, "I mean, a *real* gun?"

"It's for emergencies," Squirt explained. "The people here don't usually make a habit of taking shots at other people. Not even at illegal trespassers or criminals, which we don't often get. Not at all, really. But I don't even know where . . ."

"Yes," the Captain said, simply. "It is a gun, Evelyn."

"What is with that guy, anyway? First he didn't want to let me in, and then he did, but then he just locked me up." Before waiting for an answer, she began to answer it on her own. "Is it because he's being controlled by the Ogrimite?"

"Got it in one, Sharon," he said with a thick Australian accent.

"Sharon? My name's Evie!" She was baffled.

"Don't you watch *Kath and Kim*? I thought you would, being Australian."

Evie knew what he was talking about. She loved *Kath and Kim*. But she was still baffled. "Captain, we're running away, from a guy with a gun. Are you always this calm when your life's in danger?"

"Settle Sudan, this is nothing!" he said with a broad smile.

"Jingies," Evie muttered to herself.

Squirt had taken the lead. He knew these corridors like the back of his hand, but now he looked unsure. "Where exactly do you want to get to?"

"Out, Squirt! Out!"

He was slowing his pace, his heavy boots thudding down on the linoleum, just as they were coming up to the boss's office. "I think maybe, we should tell the boss what's going on. He could help."

"He might be watching T.V. where I suspect everyone else to be," said the Captain.

"Na, the boss never leaves his office—well, it seems like it anyway."

"Well, hurry up."

He went to knock, but the door was already about two inches open. This was a rare occurrence, and Squirt knew it. ". . . Boss? . . . Ah, boss?"

"We don't have time for this," said the Captain, quietly to himself. He and Evelyn charged forward into the boss' room.

Squirt covered his mouth in shock. It was indeed a jaw-dropping sight. Evelyn couldn't look for very long until she just had to turn her head away.

The Captain knew that it was a gun shot wound. He knew straight away, that Stretch wouldn't think twice about firing his gun at one of them. "Come on," he said softly, gently pulling Squirt away from the scene.

Squirt's brow was deeply creased. It was all that could be seen of his face. The rest was covered by his hands, and he began to whimper, from both sadness and disbelief.

The three of them walked out of there with their heads low, but after coming out through the doorway and hearing a pair of determined steady footsteps, they broke into a run.

Sometimes, in the middle of a panic, it is very easy to run and do nothing else. But we know that other things are essential to accompany the running process such as, for instance, work out which direction you are going in, decide which will be the quickest way, and most importantly, decide where you will run to and work out which turns to take in order to get there. For a few seconds, Evie, Squirt and the Captain were running aimlessly through the corridors. Their single-mindedness almost got them into trouble, for they were actually weaving themselves deeper and deeper into the building. The destination they wanted, was the exit!

Luckily, soon Squirt realised a good route they could take and quickly called out to the others, "This way!"

Evie and the Captain suddenly changed their direction causing their feet to slide along the floor, before they turned and followed Squirt.

"This is one of the ways out. I know these corridors like the back of my hand, been working here long enough! This is the back way, it'll be just as quick. Stretch probably won't expect us to be going that way!"

However, around the very next corner, their feet skidded along the linoleum floor making a high pitched screeching sound as they were forced to dig their heels in, to come to a sudden stop.

Stretch was standing, not five metres away holding the gun at them.

"Quick!" Squirt yelled. "This way!"

And the three ran in the opposite direction.

Squirt breathlessly continued, "We'll go out the front way! But we've got to be quick otherwise he'll catch up easily!"

"Won't he be expecting us to be heading for the front way now?" shouted Evie.

"Only other way!"

They ran after Squirt. He didn't hesitate once, he definitely knew where he was going. The others trusted him easily.

"Right, it's just two more corners . . ."

There was Stretch, again. Standing in front of them, blocking the way, holding up his gun.

"Quick!" Squirt yelled. "Back way!"

They disappeared around the corner from which they had just come. But before Squirt got any further, the Captain grabbed his arm and brought him to a halt.

Squirt's face said it all. He was baffled, and anxious to get to the back of the building before Stretch did.

"We're going out the front way, Squirt. Just wait. Where do you think Stretch is going now?"

"Around the ba . . . ah," said Squirt.

"I hope you're right, Captain," said Evie.

"Just wait," said the Captain. "Wait for my signal."

It was like a small group of Olympic runners eager to take off from their starting blocks, waiting for the start signal.

There were a few more seconds, then, "Now!" shouted the Captain. And they ran for it, as fast as they could go, still following Squirt.

Sure enough, Stretch had disappeared. And finally, around the next couple of corners, was the exit. They stormed through the front double doors and sprinted to the gate over a dirty, soggy yard.

"It's locked!" cried Evie, rattling the gate with both her hands.

"Squirt, do you have the key?" asked the Captain, with urgency.

Squirt had a brief look at the set of keys that were dangling around his neck, then said with shattering realisation, "No! We never get given our own key for the front and back gates. We get let out at the end of the day by a supervisor."

The Captain, after a tiny huff of frustration, began examining the gate, looking for anything he could possibly do to get himself and his companions out of there. Usually, he was really very resourceful, but this time, nothing was coming to him.

"I'm quite handy with a hair pin," Squirt said.

The Captain didn't see the point in him repeating this piece of information. "Squirt, we haven't got a . . ."

"Hair pin? I've got a hair pin!" said Evie. "I always keep a couple in my pocket in case I need them on a windy day." She reached deep inside her back jeans pocket and pulled out something that Squirt smiled at. "Is this the right sort?"

"That's perfect," he said, took it from her and began working on the lock.

Evie and the Captain were bouncing around on their toes, anxious to get out. They expected this task to take a while and feared that it would not be completed before Stretch and his gun caught up with them. But to their delight, Squirt took less than ten seconds to prize the lock undone, and together they opened up the tall, wide gate. They ran through, shutting it firmly behind them and sprinted down the muddy street.

Chapter Fifteen

The Parting Of Ways

The three escapees didn't slow their pace one little bit. It would have been too much of a risk. They couldn't see Stretch—he could have been miles away, but he could have been just around the last corner. And Evelyn's stomach sank every time she thought that he might have been just around the *next* corner, waiting for them. He seemed to be able to do that somehow back in the building.

Evie recognised all the houses they were running past, as they were the houses she'd visited briefly to try and save the occupants from being brainwashed.

She said quietly, almost breathing it out, as it was all she had the energy for, "I hope all those people are doing what I told them to do."

"Probably not," the Captain said simply. He seemed no where near as breathless as Evie. "He'll say yes, she'll say no. You say goodbye, and I say hello."

"Huh?"

Evie saw the Captain smile out the corner of her eye. Then she realised where she was and suddenly, she became the leader. "It's this way," she called, "I remember this blue stone house on the corner."

With no questions asked, the others followed her, and the Captain recognised the street as the one he and Evie were on when they had split up.

"Keep running 'till you get to the end!" said the Captain, while getting his glasses out from his inside jacket pocket and putting them on—all the while, his long coat flapping behind him.

At the end of the street, Squirt slowed to great long strides, and Evie worried that he'd collide head first into the see-through Train.

"Stop! Wait there!" she yelled.

And Squirt said, "Where are we supposed to go now?"

The Captain caught up with him, and Evelyn, not far behind. He gathered them up and said, "In here, quick."

Evie knew what to do. She knew if that she just followed the Captain, she wouldn't bump into or trip over anything. Unfortunately, Squirt didn't know so much and there were a couple of things that he bumped into and tripped over, merely from squirming and struggling untrustingly in the Captain's gentle but urgent pushes and shoves.

The Captain seemed to know exactly where to put the key and exactly where to step. Anybody doing this task should have looked ridiculous, but strangely, the Captain looked completely normal. To a passer-by, he would have looked like an impossibly brilliant mime artist—overtaking the best in the world.

Next thing, there was the Train. The sumptuous and very pleasant interior, with its wood panelling, its comfortable sofas and its intriguing patterned rug.

Evie quite enjoyed watching Squirt see the Train for the first time. She knew exactly, word for word, all the questions that were hovering on his lips. She knew what he was thinking and feeling, and what he *couldn't* say because of sheer disbelief.

The Captain had not slowed his pace, now that he was inside the Train, however. He had disappeared into the engine room and was racing around flicking switches and adjusting controls. He was about seven seconds and then he returned to where Evie and Squirt were still standing.

Then, all the questions flowed out from the excited Squirt. Evie was going to try and quickly answer them all as best she could to save the Captain the trouble, but the Captain raised a hand to shush him and interrupted—simply no time for questions.

"Right," the Captain said hurriedly. "I've set the Train on a direct course back to the Satellite. Evelyn, you'll take Squirt back there and . . . hang on," he pointed back and forth from Evie to Squirt. "Squirt, this is Evelyn, Evelyn, meet Squirt. Right, that's done. Now, the two of you will land in the same place the Train took off from. Evelyn, you think you can remember the way to the Bridge?"

"I think so, but . . ."

"Good. Take Squirt straight there. He'll know what to do to fix everything."

"Er, what exactly is the trouble?"

"Evelyn will explain everything on the way, won't you, Evelyn?"

"Yes of course, but . . ."

"You're trained in the operation and repair of the transmat mechanism and its functioning?" the Captain not exactly asked, but more so *told* Squirt.

"Yes I am," he replied, "but . . ."

"But? Why but?"

171

"Well, Evelyn's saying 'but'. I suspect she may have a concern."

The Captain turned to her. "Why but?"

"Well . . . what about the Ogrimite, Captain?"

The Captain lowered and calmed his voice. "The Ogrimite is not your only problem, no, *challenge*."

Evie said nothing and stared up at his face searching his eyes.

"Once the Train has landed up there," he continued, "it will sit there for ten minutes, and then return to Serothia."

"And then you'll come and get us," Evie said, nodding and smiling.

The Captain's face was deadly serious. "No," he said softly. "I'm staying here."

Evie's smile disappeared, "But . . . how will we get back?"

"When Squirt fixes the transmat system, he'll be able to send all those Earth people back home. Perhaps not exactly where they were taken from, but you'll find your way."

"Me?"

"Yes Evelyn, you. You're going back with them."

Evie looked neither happy, nor sad. The only change in her expression could be seen in her big black eyes.

The Captain was surprised. "You're going *home*, Evelyn. I'm getting you home. Along with your brother and your friend. Isn't that what you want?"

She stared at him for a few more seconds before her eyes drifted downward, and then she gave a quick little nod, with little commitment.

The Captain sidled past her and so now he was closest to the door, and closer to Squirt.

"Squirt," he addressed him very seriously indeed, "I'm going to try and negotiate with the Ogrimite race, try and persuade them not to take over this world, give them an alternative, I don't know—I'm going to try as hard as I can. But if they don't cooperate, if they insist on proceeding with what they've started here, I'll have no choice but to blow up Satellite SB-17."

Squirt's eyes widened, and his eyebrows turned downwards at the ends. "Blow it up? Really? Will it come to that?"

"I'm afraid so."

"But all that work. The years of planning it, designing it and building it."

"I know, and I understand the kind of effect it will have. But it's what's given the Ogrimites a foothold on your world. It's been so *easy* for them to conjure up this plan and achieve what they have because of the enormous power the Satellite has and how much Serothia relies on it."

"But I'm going to get in so much trouble!"

"Squirt, the whole planet's in trouble, if we don't do this. And it's only if the aliens refuse to cooperate with me."

"How will you do that?"

"Just leave that up to me."

"What about Stretch out there?"

"Leave him to me."

"Captain, what are the chances of them cooperating?" Evie asked.

After a short hesitation, the Captain replied gravely, "Not very big."

"Hence the ten minute return flight, eh?" said Squirt.

173

"Exactly. You and Paulo MUST BE back on board the Train in precisely ten minutes."

Squirt didn't look very confident. "Couldn't you make it longer."

"It's got to be the bare minimum time, I don't want to risk any more people getting brainwashed or sucked dry of their life. Give me some assurance that you can do this."

"In ten minutes?"

"Yes."

". . . Okay."

The Captain waited. ". . . Was that the assurance?"

Squirt nodded.

The Captain wasn't happy. "You understand, if you're not on the Train, you'll get blown up with the Ogrimite."

Squirt pointed a finger. "But only if it doesn't cooperate."

"Just a minute," said Evie, "How will they know whether you've been successful in persuasion or not, Captain? They may not have to hurry if you are."

"The portable audio clandestine digital communicator," replied the Captain.

"The *what?*"

The Captain reached forward and pulled his walky-talky thing off of Evie's waist and held it in the air. "I'll let you know how I go." He gave the device to Squirt.

With the walky-talky taken off of her, Evie suddenly felt unimportant, obsolete and finished with. Her adventure was over. She was almost invisible now. She was no longer his assistant in saving the world. She was one of the hundreds that were being rescued and sent back home. Home. Was that a bad thing? Of course not!! She missed her mum and dad, she was hungry, she was tired, she could hardly wait for Summer Camp . . . although, that was before she hopped on the Train. Now the thought of Summer Camp seemed utterly boring. But no, she was happy she was going home, back to familiar territory, back to safety. And she could do with a nice hot bath. Still . . . she couldn't help feeling disappointed though, that she would never see the Captain again, or the Train. Never see the stars up this close. Never see Paulo or Squirt again. Well how could she when they lived seventeen million light years away?

"Evie, did you catch that?" she heard the Captain say, intruding her thoughts.

"Catch what?" she said with a blank face.

The Captain couldn't believe she hadn't been listening. At the most critical time, she hadn't been listening. "I don't have time to repeat it," he said regretfully. "Squirt will have to explain on the way." He started heading out.

Evie stopped him. "Captain," she said nervously.

He turned back to her and gave her an anxious, yet tender glance.

She hesitated. She didn't exactly know what to say. ". . . Well, I'll say goodbye, then."

It was as if it was the first time the Captain had realised it. Yes, it was goodbye. His face showed an affection, which Evie was relieved of. She had wondered all along whether he had liked her and appreciated her help, or whether he never even wanted to drag her along in the first place. This look he now gave her, laid to rest all her uncertainties. *Are you coming?* He had said to her soon after they'd met. *You don't have anywhere else to go,* he'd said. Evie had thought maybe he was a mad creep after young girls and was so worried to go with him. But now, she thought to herself, she wished she'd appreciated that invitation. He was helping her, he was concerned for her. And now, she knew that well and good.

The Captain walked closer to her, and with a sad smile, she held out her hand. "Goodbye, Captain. Thank you for everything."

He shrugged this off. "For what? I haven't done much."

"Well how about, rescuing James and Lisa from certain death, saving me from being abandoned in a forgotten room, or possibly tortured by an Ogrimite pawn, showing me a little bit of this amazing universe and . . . well, making me feel . . . special. Like a hero."

The Captain appeared touched. "I'm glad you feel that way. But I hate long goodbyes so . . ."

"Yes! You've got to go and . . ."

"Save the world?"

"Save the world! Good luck. It was nice knowing you."

"You too, Evelyn. God be with you." He shook her hand vigorously, patted Squirt on the shoulder, and then hurriedly walked outside.

The door automatically shut behind him and Squirt immediately sprung into action. "Right," he said, clapping his hands loudly and making his way to the engine room.

"Do you know how to work it?" Evie asked.

"He said all I need to do, is press this button." He pointed to the button in question and pressed it straight away. Suddenly, the engine jerked into motion. Evie could hear the steam welling up and she smiled privately to herself. *Cup of tea would be really nice now—if we had the time.*

Chuff *choofety chuff, choofety* **chuff** *choofety bang! choofety* **chuff** *choofety chuff, choofety* **chuff** *choofety bang!*

The sound grew louder and louder. Evie thought how strange it was to be hearing the Train's engine, without the Captain being present. She knew the trip would be a short one, so she immediately got down to business with Squirt. But first, there was one question that had been bugging her.

"Your real name's not really Squirt, is it, Squirt?"

He smiled. "Haron. That's my real name. Haron Smeds. The nickname Squirt, I've kind of grown to like because it was sort of a term of endearment, I guess that Stretch used." At the mention of Stretch's name, Squirt's throat seemed to close up and his voice trailed off, sadly.

"Don't worry," said Evie. "Maybe the Captain's got an idea to rescue him as well. And everyone else who's been brainwashed by the Ogrimite."

"*His* real name's Marak. Marak Neeper. Hope he's going to be alright."

Evie put a comforting arm on Squirt's shoulder.

"We went through lots of training together, you know. But he'd started before me, so he finished all his tests before me. Then he became one of my trainers."

"So you've finished all your tests and everything now?"

"Yep. I've been ready to start work for a month now. Just been keeping up my knowledge and skills until I got called up. I feel like I've earned every bit of my certificate. One of the others who I sort of became friends with, he cheated on the last test. Still got the certificate. I felt so angry, 'cause I worked so hard, you know. It's a pretty huge course, and that last test, well . . . that was the big one. It doesn't seem fair does it? We both end up with the same qualification. But, I'm happy with what I've achieved."

While he was speaking, Evie's eyes had dropped from his, and she couldn't seem to look directly at him. She just nodded, and looked anywhere but into his eyes.

"You alright?" She heard him ask.

"Yep," she said with a quick nod and decided it was time they get down to business. She suddenly noticed she was hot. Not just from the running, but from her unexpected feelings of guilt, so she pulled off her hooded jacket and began. "So, what was it the Captain wanted you to explain to me?"

"Well," he sniffed, "we get up there, avoid the Ogrimite-thingy . . ."

"Somehow," Evie inserted.

". . . I fix the transmat, and we bring all the Earth people up to the Bridge."

"That's going to take ages!"

"Well . . . it just can't. Six by six they can go into the . . . what-sa-ma-call-it, matter transfer tubes, (this is rather like the test I took) and then we simply send them across."

"Do you know how many people are on that Satellite?"

"Well . . . we're going to have to move fast."

"We're going to need a miracle!"

Evie knew what had to be done, but somehow she couldn't see it happening in ten minutes. And particularly, so much moving about with an Ogrimite on board, was what was worrying her.

Chapter Sixteen

Let Your Will Be Done

Evie explained to Squirt all the troubles up on board the satellite, including the terrible obstacle known as the Ogrimite. After recapping the whole predicament, they started to perceive their task as more and more impossible.

It had not taken long at all for the Train to arrive at its destination. It had landed precisely where it had taken off. When they stepped out onto the floor of the Satellite, Squirt couldn't move. He was awestruck again at the fact that he could not see what he had just come out of. Evie shut the door behind her once she had stepped off and pulled at it to make sure it had locked.

And then Squirt, trying to forget about the impossibility of the alien space vessel, said, almost to himself, "So, this is Satellite SB-17."

"Yes," Evie said, staring into the air in front of her, and sounding drearily doubtful. "And we have ten minutes to do our job before this place blows up."

"Or not," Squirt pointed out, raising his index finger, and trying for a smile to go with it. Not wasting any more time, Squirt started moving forward, but Evie grabbed his arm to stop him. She knew better.

"Don't move," she said. "Remember, any slight move, and the Ogrimite will be able to detect us."

"Can't we just move *really* slowly?"

"*Any* movement, fast or slow. It's the same."

"But we can't stand here for ten minutes!" Squirt had set a timer on a device which looked a lot like a watch around his wrist. He glanced at it now and it said 9:43. "Nine minutes, forty-three seconds left, and counting," he said. "We don't have any choice, Evelyn. We have to move."

Hesitating, she answered, "Alright, we'll edge along here. But listen out for the Ogrimite's big loud groan that he does. That might help us work out how far away he is."

Squirt nodded, and they sidestepped all the way along the first corridor—the one Evie and the Captain had been escorted through when they arrived the first time.

After a short time, Squirt said, "I can't hear anything. This place is dead quiet."

Evie did not like his choice of words. She was scared that James and Lisa were . . .

Mmmrrrreeeeaaarrrrrgh.

Evie stopped. It was very distant. She wondered where it was, and who it was after.

There were nine minutes and nineteen seconds left on Squirt's timer.

The Captain was on his knees. He wasn't far from where the Train had taken off, and Marak Neeper was not far from catching up with him. Muddy ground did not worry him as he sat there with his head slumped, muttering quietly. If anyone had been around, they'd have thought he was destined for a loony-bin. But this was an emergency, he was seeking help.

The main subject of his muttering was that of Evelyn and Squirt. Then, as he saw Stretch's figure growing bigger and bigger as he marched closer and closer, he said a few words for a conversation he was about to have.

"Let your will be done," he finished, and then stood up to face the man with the gun.

Stretch raised his gun and took aim, ready to shoot. The Captain raised his hand and called, "Ogrimite!"

Stretch did not shoot, but he did not lower his gun either.

The Captain continued, "I want to speak to the Ogrimite who is controlling this man."

There was a pause, and then Stretch opened his mouth. "Who are you?"

"I'm the Captain," he replied.

"I command you to tell me who you are."

"You can't *command* me to do anything, I don't belong to you."

At that, Stretch prepared his gun to fire.

He knew that simply *the Captain* wasn't going to be accepted. So he quickly rephrased. "I'm Captain Georges." More was required, so he went on. "I'm a disciple of Jesus Christ—a servant of the God of the universe, and at the moment, I represent this planet."

The Captain knew he was talking to the Ogrimite himself because before Stretch spoke, there was always a pause. The Ogrimite was telling him what to say. "What is your business here?"

Inwardly, the Captain was already thanking God because the Ogrimite was listening to him. "My business here, is to appeal to you. Please don't harm the people of this planet."

"I have no wish to harm them. Only to rule them."

"Well, I'm asking you not to rule them. Do not take over this planet!"

"Your appeal is feeble, and useless. The Ogrimites will do as they please."

"But *why*? Why are you doing this? Why do you need to rule this planet?"

"Our planet was destroyed utterly by a war between two different tribes of the Ogrimite race. The war was long and devastating. There was no victory for either of us. Most just floated out to space and so nothing was resolved. There are only five million of us left scattered around the solar system in Rasca's escape ships and we have joined into one united army in order to conquer another world, on which we may live together again as we did before the war."

"Rasca was your home planet?"

"Yes."

"But why *this* world specifically. I mean, isn't there a planet in this solar system that isn't inhabited by billions of people?"

"Yes. However, they do not have the natural resources we need to survive, their atmospheres are insufficient, and we would die instantly from their temperatures."

"And let me guess, this planet offers everything suitable for you to survive in."

"It is a little warmer than Rasca, but we have spent a long time calculating the climate, and we have found that we will easily adapt. This world is ideal."

"But you can't just take someone else's world! These people are free spirits; they are not accustomed to serving alien creatures."

"They will not know they are serving us. They will not be troubled by the change."

"But that's even worse! They'll all be like your puppets, they'll have no free will!"

"What is your argument?"

The Captain sighed, frustrated. "Look, now that I know your predicament, let me give you an alternative."

"An alternative?"

"A *choice*. I understand your problem and your need for a new home. You're doing the most natural thing for all creatures great and small—you're trying to survive. But let me find you another home, not Serothia."

"We have already looked. Are you deaf?"

"Somewhere *outside* this solar system. I can travel all over the universe if I need to. There'll be somewhere you can go. Somewhere where there's no one already living. Out of the trillions and zillions of planets out there, there'll be *somewhere* you can live!"

"Our decision has already been made, and the process has already begun."

"But this is unnecessary. You don't need to brainwash people so they'll let you rule their lives. You can have your own home all to yourself! What do you say?"

After that same short pause, the Ogrimite answered, "If we take over an already inhabited world, we inherit the people on it. If we are to rebuild *our* lives, we will need help—slaves. These people on Serothia will be our slaves."

"But you can't do that to them!"

"They will not know any better."

"You're robbing their entire existence. There'll be *no* point that they were even alive!"

"Their purpose in life will be to serve us."

The Captain breathed out another frustrated puff of air. This time, however, he sounded a little defeated. "Don't you realise what I'm offering you?" he asked, softer. "I can give you a new home, without you having to worry about brainwashing anyone, making sure everyone's received the treatment, keeping them in line, keeping them fed, clothed, happy."

"They do not require these things in order to serve us."

"Yes they do, if you want them to do a good job. If they're mal-nourished, they'll just collapse and die. You'll lose hundreds of servants everyday!"

"Then we will feed them. That is no obstacle. Their happiness is not required by us."

"You still don't understand. If you choose to do this your way, and continue to take over this world, I'm going to have to stop you, because I can't let this happen."

"You are incapable of stopping us now. As we speak, I am again transmitting a message to the people of Serothia."

"But you can't be, I disconnected . . ."

"I fixed it."

"Well I knew you were clever, but I must have underestimated."

"This world is ours already. The two united tribes of Rasca are on their way to this planet and we will have this world in approximately seventeen of your Serothian minutes."

"I'll give you one more chance," he told the Ogrimite—Stretch staring back at him. "Take up my offer, or I destroy you."

"Even if you do destroy me, the two tribes of Rasca are still coming. You will have achieved nothing."

"So . . . that's a *no* then?"

"A *no*," he replied.

"Let it be."

Suddenly, to make sure this lunatic could not have the slightest chance of destroying him, Stretch was commanded to aim his weapon again and fire it with no hesitation.

The Captain had anticipated this and he grabbed the lid off the dust bin, which he had deliberately been standing next to and deflected the gun's ray of fatal ammunition. He positioned it at an angle so that Stretch himself would not be harmed—he still had hopes for that man. The strange ray of energy being shot out of the gun bounced off the dust bin lid and up into a tree on the side of the street. The tree, within seconds, came tumbling down—Stretch making a near escape from its crash on the muddy ground.

During the distraction, the Captain ran around the tree, also making a near escape from the tangled whipping of the branches, and sprinted as far as he could away from Stretch getting a head start. He was heading straight back to the broadcasting centre. It would be a long, exhausting run, so he prepared his mind for the trip.

Stretch had dived to the ground away from the falling tree and he was now picking himself up, checking that he was not hurt. He felt a powerful urge in his mind willing him to run after the crazy man. So, scooping his gun up into his arm, he ran after the Captain.

The sound was not heard again. It was the instinct of Squirt to believe that this was a good thing, however, Evie knew that it was not that simple. Squirt thought that it must have meant that the Ogrimite was too far away to be heard, but all Evie knew, was that no sound, meant no indication of where it was. It could be five miles away, or it could be five metres away.

Even though they had been moving at a snail's pace, they had almost reached the doorway which led to the ladder, which led to the lower chambers.

"That's where Paulo has all the Earth people, for safe-keeping," Evie said softly. "The monster could be down there. Or it could be up at the Bridge. Or after us. Who knows?" Evie was clearly in a panic. She read eight minutes and forty-seven seconds on Squirt's timer. She knew that the task ahead of them, was just impossible. Simply impossible, and she thought again of the idea of never ever seeing her family again, nor her friends, school, teachers, church, or the Simpsons ever again.

She tried not to think about it. She tried to focus on the Ogrimite, tried to work out what it could be doing and where. But this was also impossible. There was no way of telling. Everything was silent. Everything except for her heart beat, her heavy breathing, (which she was trying to suppress for fear that it was making too much movement), and of course the footsteps.

Footsteps? Running footsteps! *What on Earth? That person has a death wish! No . . . it's at least two people.*

Suddenly, there were three fast moving bodies skidding around the corner, almost crashing head first into Evie and Squirt.

"Evie!" shouted James, as soon as he saw her. He hugged her. "You're okay! Where have you been? How did you get back here?"

Evie said quickly, "Yes, with the Captain, by Train."

James looked confused. "Again with the train.

"Look, never mind the Train, where's the Ogrimite?" she asked.

"We think it's gone to do another transmission." Then he said sadly, "Another few people died. That's where it got the energy to transmit again. When it runs out of energy, it'll come back out for more. And the whole process is just going to go round and round and . . ."

"*He*."

"What?"

"It's a *he*, not an *it*. And who are your friends?" she said looking at James' two running companions.

"This is Hans," he said patting the skinny business man on the arm, then he knelt down by the little girl, "and this is Moira. I'm taking them to the chambers. Paulo asked me to."

"Keep them," said Squirt, with authority. "We've got to get all those people down there back to a planet called Earth and we've only got . . . eight minutes and thirty-one seconds to do it!"

"But, we can't *send* them back, we've been trying, but . . ."

"What do you think *I'm* here for?"

"Quick," Evie said, "Hurry up, while the Ogrimite's busy! Let's bring 'em up!"

Evie sprung into action. She ran straight to the door, which led to the chambers, which led to the Earth people, turned the wheel lock with great force and just about jumped down that ladder.

James had many questions, but he saved them. He knew better than to waste precious time. Even though one of his questions was, *why do we only have eight minutes and thirty-one seconds?*

By the time Evelyn opened the wheel lock of the first chamber, Squirt's timer said: 8:22

Chapter Seventeen

What 'Impossible' Looks Like

The Captain was slowly beginning to question whether he'd taken the right turn. The broadcasting centre wasn't all that far away, but there were multiple twists and turns along the way, and the suburban streets of Serothia (or at least this part of Serothia) were not laid out in the conventional way. Sharp corners were there where you least expected them to be, and where you might expect to see a driveway, there were none in sight.

Nevertheless, the Captain still had Shemas's directions in his head—he could still hear his voice. So he commanded the doubts to leave his mind* and he kept on running in the direction he was going, confidently.

Soon, another thought entered his mind. In approximately eight minutes, he was going to blow up Satellite SB-17. And in approximately eight minutes, Squirt and Paulo had to get out of there before the time was up. The Captain's thought was this: How could he be sure that Paulo and Squirt's eight minutes was the same as his own eight minutes? They had not synchronised

---

*   By saying something like, "Get behind me Satan!"

their watches.♦ He decided to use a life-line. The device, which Evie had called a walky-talky.

"What's that crackling noise?" James asked, helping an old lady up the ladder from the chambers.

"I know that sound," Evie said.

"Sounds like a radio of some sort," said Squirt, quite bemused.

"The radio!" Evie suddenly shouted.

"The what?" said Squirt.

"The walky-talky . . . thing!" she was pointing to his overalls pocket.

"Huh?"

Evie, thinking they would have been much better off if the Captain had have left the device with her, reached for Squirt's pocket, and grabbed the walky-talky.

"Oh!" said Squirt.

"Hello?" said Evie. "Captain?"

The voice on the other end definitely belonged to the Captain. He asked if Squirt was there.

Evie put on a tired expression and held out the walky-talky to Squirt. "It's for you."

Evie heard him say something about making sure they had exactly the same time. Squirt's timer displayed: 8:11 and the Captain adjusted his watch accordingly.

"Remember," the Captain was finishing, "by the time your timer reaches zero, you *must be* on the Train! The whole satellite *must be* empty!"

"Except for the Ogrimite."

♦ Which meant, of course, to make sure that the Captain's watch and Squirt's timer were on exactly exactly exactly the same time.

"You got it."

"So, I guess the Captain's reasoning didn't work, then," said Evie after Squirt had replaced the walky-talky to his pocket.

"I guess not," replied Squirt. "Come on, we've got a lot to do."

"You go up to the Bridge and start fixing the transmat!" said Evie. "We'll send everyone up to you."

"Good idea," Squirt said rushing up the ladder. "But hurry up, we only have eight minutes!"

The passageway leading from the first chamber to the ladder, was filled with noise. So much noise, Evie had to shout at James, who was standing right next to her, to be heard. "This is the weirdest thing I've ever done!"

James was shouting at all the confused people in the chamber to hurry up and get out of there. "No one's going to believe us when we get back home!" he then said.

Lisa had joined them now and both her and James were hurrying people out of the chambers and to the ladder, while Evelyn decided to climb the ladder herself and be the one to make sure they all got to the Bridge. It was not long until the passage way and the corridor above were packed with people, all heading in one direction. There was not a lot of need to direct them, because it had become one continuous stream of people following the people in front. They looked like a sea of sheep all being led hurriedly from one place to another. Except, these people were being taken to be rescued, rather than being led to the slaughter.

All Evie tried to do was to reassure people that everything was going to be okay. She shouted constantly that this was their way out and back home. Some believed her and had thankfulness written all over their faces.

However, some did nothing but complain or believed they were being tricked and so tried to go against the current of the moving mass of people.

Now that Squirt was no longer with her, Evie had no idea how much time they were taking. How much time they had left until Satellite SB-17 was no more. Then she began to wonder how the Captain was supposed to be able to blow up the satellite. *He must have a plan. And he must have really tried hard to reason with the Ogrimite before deciding to blow it up. Otherwise, he's just a murderer.*

The Captain recognised something. At last, there was something that assured him he was going the right way. It was just a tree, but a particularly shaped tree. He looked up into its twisted branches. The funny way it curled around itself and then hung dangerously over the road. It made him run faster, with a new energy. Knowing he wasn't far away.

Something else that was not far away was the man with the gun. He knew Serothian weapons were primitive, but they were sufficient and could easily kill a man. Stretch walked, while the Captain ran. But somehow, he still managed to keep up. He walked with enormous strides, and his calm, confident manner was all the more frightening.

On his way past windows of houses, the Captain could see people watching their televisions, and he groaned. On their screens was snowy nothingness, with occasional blue flickers, that the viewers seemed so entranced by. All the Captain could do, was run past them. And he convinced himself that there must be a way the brainwashing can be reversed. He did not, however, wish to underestimate the Ogrimite's power and capabilities.*

Only two more streets, he thought, *and then I'm there.* He looked down at the watch on his left wrist. Another half a minute had gone.

7:41

Squirt had finally got through the thick crowd and reached the Bridge. As part of his training, he had studied diagrams and maps of Satellite SB-17. He knew the whole place like the back of his hand. He could walk through the place blindfolded and know exactly where everything was. In the Bridge, he found a young man, a little younger and shorter than himself.

"Who are you?" Paulo exclaimed, alarmed.

"My name's Haron Smeds. I'm a technician. I'm here to fix the matter transfer system."

To Squirt's surprise, Paulo suddenly dropped to his knees in relief and raved, "Oh thank you, thank you! I can't believe this! Oh thank you."

"Surely, there's no time to waste! There are people on their way now to be sent home. In seven minutes and thirty-five seconds, this Satellite is going to be blown to smithereens."

"What?!!"

"No time to explain," Squirt said. Then he added on his way to repair the machinery, "which is unusual for me."

---

* He'd done this once before with another individual with power—much much more power than that of an Ogrimite. It was what changed his life.

As soon as he started work, there were people surging through the doorway to the Bridge. Paulo could do nothing but try and organise them into a line, and try to explain. "Now, please try and keep calm. The transmat system is being repaired and very soon, you will all be able to go home!"

"You mean we're going back into those tube things?" yelled a tall podgy man wearing a tank top and a number of tattoos.

"Yes. It's your only way back to Earth!"

"Earth?" said Squirt.

Paulo turned around. "Well, yes. These people come from Earth."

"Oh I know, I just don't think I know any coordinates for that place."

"The coordinates should still be there. It's where they were all coming from. You've got to be able to get them back, you've just *got* to!"

"The coordinates would only be for the very last place of origin, will that do?"

"I guess it'll be where that tall man came from. Yes, that'll do. We've just got to get them out of here. How long will you be?"

"What's going on? What's the hold up?" yelled a teenaged boy from the swarm.

"Please, try and be patient," said Paulo, a little worried. "We'll get you home. How long?" he then demanded of Squirt.

"Seven minutes, twenty seven."

"What?! But you said this place will blow up in . . ."

"Yeah, that's what I meant," he said, standing up, clapping his hands together to brush off the dust. "Oh you meant, how long will it take to repair the system?"

"Yes."

Squirt gestured towards the tubes and smiled "All yours."

Paulo's gratitude was written all over his face. "You're a genius."

"Well, come on. We've got no time to lose."

Both he and Paulo approached the group bulging at the doorway saying, "Come on, quickly. Six at a time. One, two, three, four, five, six, go. Get in. Trust us. Have a nice trip. Oh, and you'll have to find your own way once you get there."

One lady already in the tubes asked worriedly, "What do you mean?" But in a flash of light at the flick of Paulo's wrist, the woman was gone, along with the five others lined next to her.

"Right, next six!" called Squirt.

And they carried on in this way diligently, while Squirt's timer ticked onto 7:13.

Moving past Evie now, there was a more constant flow of people. She assumed this to mean that Squirt had managed to start sending people back home. She wished she could talk to the Captain, just for a few moments, to ask him exactly what he was going to do. There was so much she didn't understand. If she knew just a little bit more, perhaps she'd find it easier to trust him. At that moment, a thought hit her like a sixteen tonne weight. This is what her brother's youth leader was on about the other week about God. If she *did* know more, she would find it not easier, but *unnecessary* to trust him. But then she thought and worried about all these poor innocent people around her, and herself for that matter, and thought, *what's the good of trust? It's just frustrating. I wanna know!*

She got another "What's going on?" from the crowd.

"You're going home," she answered.

"Why should I trust you?" he asked angrily.

She was taken aback. She felt so small, so young, and so useless. Then she thought to say, "Because you've got no other choice." Her words were just as much for her, as they were for the man.

Squirt and Paulo had put through nine loads of people. Fifty-four people, all back to Earth, safe and sound.

Squirt looked at the timer on his wrist.

Paulo asked, "How much time do we have left?"

"Six minutes fifty-one," he replied flatly, quickly becoming exhausted.

Shoving the last of another six people into the tubes and pressing the activation button, Paulo said doubtfully, "We're never going to get through them in time."

Squirt pulled the Captain's walky-talky out of his pocket again. "Captain? Come in, Captain. Do you read me?"

After a short fuzzy, crackling noise, came the Captain's voice. "Yes Squirt, I read you, what is it?"

"We've got under seven minutes left and we've only got sixty people back to Earth."

"Sixty, that's great," said the Captain. "You got it working then, keep going."

"Yeah but, we're never going to get there in time."

"Never say never. Well, not in that context, anyway."

"But since we've got the radio communication, couldn't we just keep in contact, like . . . couldn't I contact you when we've got everyone home and *then* you blow up the Satellite?"

"Squirt, in case you've forgotten, I set the Train on an automatic return flight. Whether you're in that Train or not when the time's up, it's coming back to Serothia."

"Why didn't you just set it for a longer time, then?"

"Because it's very likely that the Ogrimite on board Satellite SB-17 has already sent for his friends to come and drop in on the lovely Serothia and I estimate that in just over seven minutes, they'll be ready to land. The Ogrimite already has control over hundreds, maybe thousands of people. Brainwashing the Serothian people is more or less the battle, as soon as the Ogrimite colony land, this planet is as good as theirs! The hard bit's already been accomplished."

"But we've only done sixty . . ." There was another flash of light, ". . . sixty-six people, I don't think . . ."

"It's alright, just have faith. You'll get there."

"But Paulo said there were about fifteen hundred people on board. Now it takes about five seconds for six people to get into the tubes and be zapped back to Earth. I've calculated that to get through everybody, it would take seven thousand, five hundred seconds, which is one hundred and twenty-five minutes. Captain, that's approximately two hours! You gave us ten minutes! We're going to need a miracle to do this!"

"That's exactly what I'm depending on," said the Captain. "See you soon. Over and out."

Squirt was watching, as Paulo had sent another two lots through. He looked at his timer. 6:40. "He's crazy."

"Who?"

"The Captain. He's going to blow us all up."

"Just let's concentrate on this, shall we?" Paulo thought of the Captain as quite a level-headed man. Even though he knew this task was pretty crazy, somehow, he managed to keep going. Somehow, he managed to trust the Captain.

Mmmrrrreeeerrrrrgh, came a distant sound. Paulo looked up with dread.

"Was that the . . ." asked Squirt.

"Ogrimite," Paulo nodded. "That could mean he's on the move again."

"Which means we ought *not* to be on the move."

"Exactly."

"But we have fourteen hundred and twenty-eight more people to get back to Earth."

"Not that many," Paulo said with a serious, solemn face. "Some have already perished."

"Let me through! I'm not dying here in this weird unknown place, I want to get home!" A lady was pushing her way through to the front of the crowd towards the tube.

"So do I, let me into one of those things," shouted a man.

Soon, everyone was pushing their way to the front, trying to beat everyone else to one of the tubes. Squirt was at the tubes and he looked over the top of the crowd (because he was nice and tall) at Paulo with a worried, questioning look.

Paulo shouted over the noise. "Just let them in, I'm going to send them. But only one to a tube!"

"I know, I know!" Squirt let six people forward into the tubes. But one woman pushed through screaming, "I don't want to die! I don't want to die!" And she squeezed into a tube with the younger girl who was already in there. And before Squirt could stop him, Paulo pressed the button and the blinding light flashed. Five people had disappeared. But the two in the one tube remained, and with them in the tube were sparks and little curls of smoke rising from the base.

The older woman came out and demanded of Squirt angrily, "What went wrong? Why didn't it work?"

Squirt said sullenly, "You exhausted the circuits. The tubes can't take more than one person." Then, guiding the two ladies to two separate tubes and three others into the three remaining tubes, Squirt said, absolutely hopelessly, "We now have only five working transmat beams."

Chapter Eighteen

That Stupid Whistle

There it was. The broadcasting centre. He ran towards the doors for the second time that day without stopping, Stretch still not far behind. Once again, the Captain had no problem getting past the front reception area. Everyone was glued to a television monitor. There were monitors everywhere. Up in the corner of every room. Anyone working there would have no chance of not being drawn in by the Ogrimite's broadcast. Becoming frustrated at the sight, he stood there for a few seconds trying to think how he would undo what the Ogrimite was doing. Stretch had no recollection of who he was before. None of these people will either.

But there was a fine line between the Captain stopping there and thinking, and the Captain slowly paying attention to the hypnotising screen. He could hear the soft gentle buzz of the static. He could see the even rhythmic pulses of the flickering blue light. The more he listened to it, the more he tuned in, and it slowly began to make a strange sort of sense in his mind. He felt calm. Like he was about to not have to worry about anything. All he had to do was let go.

Let go . . .

No.

It was thanks to the sound of a gun shot that brought his worries back. He felt a heavy burden on him all of a sudden, but he was grateful for that burden. When he realised the gun shot was Stretch coming closer, he could hardly believe he had almost been lost in the snowy static secrets of the television screen just seconds ago. And he ran with imaginary blinkers on each eye, forcing himself not to stop and look at one of those screens. He ran straight to the room where he was before. One of the news rooms, which he knew had the main receiver on top of it. He pushed past a number of dazed people—none of them even caring who he was or why he was there. They weren't even bothered that they had been shoved by the Captain as he brushed past them.

And when he found the room he was after, he found the news desk there, a big camera pointing directly at it, and his wonderful invention to stop Ogrimite transmission from the satellite to Serothia—completely destroyed.

"Oh well," sighed the Captain, "short term solutions never did anyone any harm. As long as they're followed up with a long term solution."

He ran to the other end of the room, past the news desk, where there was an 'EXIT' sign all lit up in yellow and red. He barged through the door underneath it and he found day light, and a flight of metal, mesh steps. He ran up them, two at a time and at the very top, which was just one more floor up was what he was looking for. On the roof of the broadcasting centre, a giant satellite dish sat, absolutely enormous and it had been *just* visible from the road

A broad grin spread across the Captain's face. He looked at his watch. Five minutes and forty-eight seconds left.

Mmmrrrreeeerrrrrgh!

Evelyn heard the sound from where she was at the top of the ladder and she started to tremble in fear. Then she worried for all the people moving past her. There was so much movement, constantly. How would she ever convince them to stop? Not all of these people had seen what the Ogrimite could do. They were all determined to get home. They were promised that that's where they were going. She imagined that nothing in the world could stop them.

She had to try. "Stop!!" she shouted, louder than she'd ever shouted before. It seemed that nobody heard. Not even those who were passing right in front of her. But of course they heard. They just didn't want to stop. "Stop walking!! Stay absolutely still!!"

Nobody took any notice.

Mmmrrrreeeerrrrrgh!!

Evie was sure it sounded closer, and she started to panic. With this much movement going on, they'd have no chance. She *must* get their attention. Then, all of a sudden, she remembered something. She rushed through the crowd as fast as she could and climbed halfway down the ladder.

"James!" she called out.

He turned around and shouted over the noise of the people. "What?"

"The whistle!"

"What?"

"The *whistle!!* Tell me you've still got it!"

He reached into his pocket and then after a small pause, nodded.

"Throw it to me!"

"What?"

"Chuck it here!!"

He tossed it without any questions.

It was a good catch. Then Evie climbed back up, ran out in front of a big clump of people and blew hard on the whistle. It was ear piercing. Everyone on board the satellite, with a sense of hearing, would have heard it.

James heard it down below. She could drive him crazy with that stupid whistle.

The noise died completely. She had their attention. But they hadn't stopped moving.

"Please," she shouted, "listen to me. You've got to stay still."

Then, as if on cue, the Ogrimite moaned. *Mmmrrrreeeerrrrrgh!!*

"That noise," Evie said, "is an Ogrimite and it's sensitive to movement. If it detects our movement, it'll come after us and drain us of our energy and all our life and that, and we'll die!"

A little girl somewhere in the crowd started to cry. Other than that, the place was silent. Just when Evie thought they'd taken her seriously, and were about to do as she'd said; the crowd suddenly burst into laughter.

She frowned and felt so frustrated, she wanted to blow up and then they'd all die from her explosion. She tried the whistle again and shouted out, "I'm serious. What do you think that sound was, then? Listen to me! I'm trying to save your lives!"

"She is right!" shouted a woman suddenly from the crowd. She had a Polish sounding accent. She quietened the crowd a bit by repeating, "She's right!!" Then she looked at Evie as she made her way towards her. "I believe you." She joined Evie where she was standing in front of everyone and then faced the people. "I saw the Ogrimite. It just looks like a big blue blob, but it's deadly. It killed a man right in front of my eyes. We stopped moving like the girl and some men told us to do, and it fled from us!"

There was mumbling from the crowd.

The woman said, "It's our only chance of survival."

Then, to Evie's surprise and delight, the people in front of her stopped trying to push and shove and stayed relatively calm. These people were not aware that in about five minutes the whole satellite was going to be blown up. Evie decided to keep this piece of information to herself for now.

The constant flow had stopped. There were still people clogging up in the hallway at the top of the ladder.

"I know what's happened," James said, after Lisa had asked him. "They've all stopped moving, because of that Ogrimite sound we heard earlier. We'd better do the same."

"But the time!"

"I know, I know." Then he said quietly, "Lord, we really need you to step in right now. We can't do this on our own."

"Is that it?" Squirt asked, confused. He looked out beyond the door of the Bridge. "Is that everyone?"

"No," Paulo replied, also confused. "There should be loads more."

Mmmrrrreeeerrrrrgh!!

"Quick, shut the Bridge door!" Paulo suddenly said.

"But . . . the people . . ."

"Evelyn must have gotten them to stop. That Ogrimite will devour them if they don't. And it'll devour us if you don't close the door."

Squirt did so, locking a large group of noisy, impatient people on the Bridge with them. Paulo continued to escort people to the five functioning transmat beams.

"But there's so much movement in here. What if it can get through the door?" Squirt shouted.

"It hasn't yet. And until we know that it can, we're going to keep working in here."

After hurriedly shoving a few more groups into the tubes, Squirt wiped his brow with his sleeve and said, "Whoo, it feels like we've been doing this much longer than ten minutes."

"What does your timer say?" Paulo said urgently.

"Five thirty-five."

Big world, small satellite. Although SB-17 was big, it was a mere speck compared to Serothia itself. The television and radio broadcasting station was also bigger than the satellite and its capabilities went beyond beaming transmissions up to it. It had the capacity for an enormous amount of power, yet the satellite could only contain so much. Now, the Captain figured that if the satellite's radio transmissions were relayed, not out all over Serothia, but back down to the broadcasting centre, a continuous loop would form and signals would keep bouncing back and forth from one to the other (and with a little special jiggery-pokery of the Captain's tools in the system), eventually the satellite would be overloaded with the power from the broadcasting centre and Serothia could say bye-bye to it, as well as to the Ogrimite on board. The amount of power would be too much for the vessel to contain and . . . well . . . poof. This would be a visual representation to the approaching Ogrimite army that Serothia was defended and that the Serothian people will not allow invaders! In other words, it would hopefully scare the Ogrimites off.

This was the Captain's plan, and it was the only plan he had. So right now, he was rushing back down the steps and barged *in* through the exit door to begin his jiggery-pokery.

Evie stood frozen, straining her ears to hear the Ogrimite groan again. When it didn't, she grew all the more nervous.

When it did, her heart jumped up into her throat. The people in front of her were fidgeting nervously, and although she could tell they were doing it almost subconsciously, she reminded them not to move a muscle.

One good thing always seemed to come with a bad with this Ogrimite. The good thing was that Evie was sure it sounded further away suddenly. The bad thing was, it meant it was probably after the others in the Bridge. She wondered suddenly whether the Ogrimite had figured out how to unlock the Bridge doorway. It didn't have one second of trouble with the wheel locks on the chamber's doors. The Bridge door was different, more complex . . . Evelyn tried to reassure herself.

"Lord," she suddenly said underneath her breath. "If you can hear me, and if you're the huge, amazing God that James keeps saying you are, you'll keep that Ogrimite from getting into the Bridge. In fact, why couldn't you kill it on the spot? Bring down a lightening bolt and . . . that might kill us too." She then felt pretty stupid and said to herself, "There aren't any clouds out there, this is space, remember?" She continued talking to God: "Can't it just . . . drop dead. If you've got so much power, that'd be easy wouldn't it?" Then a thought came to her, "You probably created that thing, so you'd probably prefer to do anything but kill it." Then another thought came to her. "I know! God, couldn't you make time go really slow or something. Or speed us up really fast without us even knowing it, that'd be so coo . . ."

"Mummy! Where mummy? I want to go home!" There was a small boy, only about three years old, walking around and looking up at the people around him. He had broken the nervous silence. "I want to go home. What going on? Where mummy?"

Evie gasped, her mouth dropped open. The boy was waving his arms in the air, and then trying to run through the crowd of people. Grown ups around him were trying to hold him still, but it seemed that the more they did, the more he wriggled and jerked away.

Evie looked worriedly around, where the sound of the Ogrimite had come from, and then she raced quickly to the boy and asked him his name.

"I want mummy and daddy. Where mummy and daddy?"

"Mummy and daddy aren't here at the moment," she said gently, crouching down so they were face to face. "What's your name?" she asked again.

"Daniel."

"Okay, Daniel, tell you what. While we're waiting for mummy and daddy, we're playing a game, all of us. Do you want to play?"

He sheepishly nodded with his finger in his mouth and a tear not far from escaping.

"Okay, what you have to do is stay absolutely still, okay."

He nodded again, lightening up a bit.

"And if you move, that means you . . . you lose points! Okay?"

Again, he nodded, more enthusiastically this time.

Evie stood up straight and stayed next to him, without moving.

"Who watching?" Daniel blurted out.

"What?"

"Who watching us moving?"

"Oh, who's judging? To see who moves? Everyone. Everyone around you is judging. So if you move," she animated her voice. "there's sure to be someone who sees you."

It had worked. Evie felt quite pleased. Then she remembered the dilemma. People were getting restless, it wasn't just Daniel. In fact, Daniel was now doing the best job of staying still.

"I'll be right back," Evie said to Daniel, and she crept back through to the front of the crowd.

Mmmrrrreeeerrrrrgh!!

She stopped. Waited. Then, she started to part from the group, moving a little way up the corridor in the direction of the Bridge.

When she had just disappeared around the corner, a man yelled out, "If a little girl can go ahead, I'm going too!" And he charged forward through the crowd. He had followers, who agreed with him and charged forward as well, sounding like an angry mob about to invade a castle.

"No!!" said the woman who had helped Evie before, "No, don't move!! What are you doing?"

Some were staying still, and panicking. Others had run along behind the man. Some didn't know what to do. And Daniel was shouting, "You moved, you moved, you moved, you moved!"

Evelyn couldn't believe what had happened. The running people almost trampled on her like a stampede. She hastily got out her whistle again and blew on it hard.

It simply had no effect this time. No one wanted to listen. A large group of people, led by the first impatient man, stormed past her and she could do nothing about it.

"They'll get us all killed," she heard that woman say.

All Evie could do was blow on the whistle. So she did, and she didn't stop. Maybe the people will realise the urgency if she kept blowing. That was her only hope.

Mmmmrrrrreeeeeaaaaarrrrrgh!!!!

Suddenly, the sound was so loud, it drowned out the whistle. And it was followed by many many screams. Before Evie had time to think, she saw, from just around the corner, amongst the impatient mob, bodies falling to the ground—drained of life, pale faced and limp. It almost looked like a game of dominos played by a cold and sadistic giant—using humans for the pieces.

Following this, was the inevitable. The glowing, gliding, untouchable Ogrimite. And when it wailed, Evelyn had to cover her ears.

Chapter Nineteen

Home Run

While things up in the satellite were frantic, down on Serothia, the Captain sat still in a chair in the news room, his elbows resting on the desk in front of him and his forehead resting on his one-inside-the-other fists. Although he looked defeated, he was far from it. He had done all he could and now he was asking again for intervention. For something that he, himself could not do. Everything was ready. He watched his watch. 4:02, 4:01, 4:00, 3:59 . . .

Evie had slumped against the wall behind her. She was losing her strength. She felt her limbs beginning to wilt, her eyelids, becoming droopy. She could hear that same woman calling to the others, "Don't move! Can't you see what it's doing? If you want to live, stop moving!"

The voice sounded distant and soon, Evie realised that her hearing was dissolving—her vision beginning to blur. She could see the Ogrimite in front of her. You would think she would be trying to think up some way of getting herself out of danger. But all that was running through her head was *blow the whistle. Blow the whistle.*

She could feel its shape in her right hand, and her fingers managed to establish a firmer grip. She sluggishly lifted her head so that her and the Ogrimite were face to sort-of-face. Then she found just the necessary strength to lift her right arm and place the whistle between her lips. Staring straight ahead at the giant blue brute, she took the biggest breath she could manage and blew hard. But Evie's *hard* was not very hard at all. She was convinced this would be her last breath and that this was her last moment alive. She had done all she could and it hadn't been enough. There she was, feebly blowing a whistle in front of the enemy who was to be her killer. When she couldn't blow any more, her eyes shut, she collapsed onto the floor, and the whistle fell from her hand. Everything was black and she could feel nothing.

It was this girl. She did something . . . I don't know what, but the blue thing fled. What happened to that lot though? I haven't the faintest idea, but they're definitely dead. Looked like they just got weaker and weaker until . . . but what about that girl, is she alright? Well she's alive, I can tell you that much. That thing is still here somewhere though, we probably should keep still. Still? Yes, still. No, I mean we still have to not move? Yes! I don't reckon we're clear of it yet, this girl just got it away somehow.

Evie was slowly waking up. She tried opening her eyes. Her eyelids had never felt heavier.

I think she's waking up. Well that's a relief, I wasn't sure whether I remembered the first aid procedure for an unconscious person.

Her eyelids fluttered, until she could see light. And then some blurry shapes not far away from her.

Do you think we should help her up?

We don't want to move too much.

"She'll need a hand though. That thing is probably a long way away." A woman's voice.

"Do we know her name?" A man's voice.

"No I don't. Perhaps I'll try asking her."

The blurred shapes started to take the form of human figures. One crouched down by her.

"What's your name, young lady?" asked the woman. "Can you hear me?"

Evie felt something warm clasp onto her hand.

"Young lady? Can you hear me? Nod if you can hear me."

Evie managed to give a slight nod.

"Can you feel me holding your hand?"

She nodded again.

"Tell me your name, why don't you," the lady said kindly.

Evie started to see some defined features on the woman's face. It was the woman with the Polish accent who had helped her keep everyone still. She managed to clear her throat and push out her voice. "Evie," she said.

"Evie," the woman smiled. "You're a hero."

"That's the lot, we need to get some more people through!" said Squirt worriedly.

Paulo stood still and quiet, listening for the Ogrimite. "I haven't heard it wail recently, have you?"

"No," replied Squirt. "What if it's waiting for us on the other side of that door?"

Paulo clicked his tongue in annoyance. He didn't want to hear that kind of talk. Thinking that they would just have to open it and find out, he headed for the door and listened again. Suddenly, he looked back at Squirt, managing a smile. "I can hear people coming." He didn't hesitate to open the door. Down the corridor a little, Evie was leading a pack of people but she looked somewhat confused. She was accompanied by a middle-aged gentleman in a suit and woman of a similar age but wearing young fashionable clothes. They appeared to be helping Evie walk along. Paulo frowned and worried for her.

"What do you mean I scared it off?" Evie asked of her two escorts.

"You blew a whistle with what looked like your last breath, and the Ogrimite just . . . fled. It didn't hesitate. After what seemed to be a little cry of pain, it just turned around and disappeared around the corner. We haven't heard from it since."

"It's a *he* by the way. And you're telling me that my feeble little blow on the whistle . . . that must have been some whistle blow."

"No. No, no, that is it, I could hardly hear it."

"I didn't hear it at all," said the man.

"I probably heard it only because I was watching you. The sound wouldn't have scared a mouse."

"It must have been that particular sound that scared it, I don't know," said the man.

Evie then said softly to herself, brow creased with puzzlement. "But Ogrimites can't hear *anything*."

They were just meeting Paulo in the doorway to the Bridge. He hustled them in extremely quickly. He had gotten the hang of dealing with terrified, home-sick people by now.

The woman who had Evie on her arm told Paulo what had happened after he'd asked. Then Evie slumped into Paulo's arms saying how she couldn't understand what she'd done.

"Perhaps you'd better lie down, Evie," Paulo said.

"You *know* the Ogrimite doesn't have a sense of hearing, so what scared it off? It might have been something bigger and more dangerous . . ."

"Look, we can't worry about that now, I have to get these people home."

"Yes of course." She started heading back out the door.

"Where are you going?"

"Well to guide the people here."

"You should lie down!"

"No, I'm getting my strength back, it's alright. I just need air. I need to get out of this room, it's filled with people."

He grabbed her arm. "The corridor's filled with people as well. Where's the Ogrimite now? Are we safe for a while?"

"I have no idea." She was sounding a little bit more lively.

Paulo called out over the crowd. "Time, Squirt?"

"Three minutes, twelve!"

Paulo looked at the vast sea of people on the Bridge yet to go home. Then he glanced out onto the vast river of people streaming through the corridor. "How are we ever going to do this?" he said to himself.

"Are you sure that was the last chamber?" James called to Lisa after he'd helped the last person up the ladder.

"Yes, I know it was."

"Right, we'd better get on the end of the line, then." James grabbed Lisa's hand and helped her up the ladder. After taking one last glance of the unusual place, he hopped on and climbed after her. Once they reached the top, they hit a wall of people. They couldn't move another step forward for quite a while.

"This is like lining up for a showbag at the show," James said.

Lisa found it hard to smile at his joke. She couldn't help thinking . . . "James, do you think we'll get there in time?"

"'Course," he said without looking at her.

"But so much time has already passed. Surely the ten minutes will be up any second."

James glanced at his watch, equally worried, but not showing it. "We've still got about three minutes I think."

Lisa swallowed a head-jerking swallow. Her body was itching, bursting to move forward. She had to contain the desire to run ahead of everyone and get to the Bridge quicker. Energy was racing through her legs and feet, but she kept still, and it was torture. Soon, they moved forward about a foot. In another little while, they would move forward another foot, and so on.

In what felt like half an hour, the Bridge was filled with the very last batch of Earth people from the chambers. James and Lisa were on the end and they finally reunited with Evelyn.

"After this lot, we can go home," Lisa said, happy, but underneath, still worried they weren't going to make it.

Evelyn nodded, but didn't smile or show any enthusiasm.

"Don't worry, Evie," James said, reassuring her. "I'm sure we'll get there in time." James decided not to look at his watch. In fact, he utterly refused to.

At James' comment, Evie nodded again, but still with no smile or enthusiasm. The cause of her blandness was not because she was worried they weren't going to make it.

Squirt had a new found energy for hustling people into the tubes. Being able to see the end of the line, made him work faster and with more hope. They were nearing the end and the satellite hadn't even blown up yet!

Paulo was beginning to smile as well. He didn't care to know what the time was either for fear of losing a few seconds in the process of finding out. *Just do it*, he thought, *we're on the home run now. Just keep working!*

The Earth people couldn't seem to move fast enough. There was pushing and shoving—most of it unintentional. People were tripping over other people's feet, someone accidentally pulled a girl's hair, one lady got accidentally poked in the eye, a boy of eight almost got trampled on by a walking stick, one poor old woman was trying very hard not to let her bath robe slip, and one unfortunate short little gentleman kept getting pushed into the back of a very tall, fat lady. I still feel sorry for him, even to this day.

It was one chaotic commotion, but luckily, the numbers kept on decreasing, for they were, five at a time, being zapped back to Earth. Things were looking up. No one knew how much time they had left, but they all began to have a real honest hope, of making it out of this disaster.

It was Evelyn, who had been making her way through the turbulent crowd to sneak a quick glance at Squirt's timer. And she swallowed hard. It was ticking steadily: 1:38, 1:37, 1:36 . . .

Mmrrreeerrrrrgh.

Evie looked up at Squirt. And he looked down at her.

"Oh no," Squirt said. "Please no."

"Where's Evie?" James suddenly said, worriedly. "Where's Evie?" he shouted. The sound of his voice was just swallowed up by the loud hollering from all the people.

Lisa was looking around in a panic. "She was here a second ago. What if she's out there with the thing?"

"Why would she go out there?"

Mmmrrrreeeerrrrrgh!

"It's come back," Squirt said with dread. "Is that Bridge door closed?"

"Yes. We were *just* able to then. Do you think the door will stop him?"

Squirt thought for a moment. Then he swallowed. "We'll just have to hope so."

Evie thought about this for a couple of seconds. 1:23, 1:22 . . .

"That's not good enough," she said and then immediately pushed her way back again through the crowd. This time, she was going against the grain* but nothing could stop her.

Squirt had a puzzled look on his face as he closed another tube door.

"Evie wouldn't risk going out there!" James said. "And for what?"

"The only thing I can think of is that she'd go out there to try and distract the Ogrimite, stop it from coming in here."

"What, risk her life for other people? I can't picture little Evie doing something like . . ."

"Coming through!" said Evie on her way past Lisa and her brother. She ran straight into the Bridge door, unlocked it and bolted through.

"Evie!" James yelled, "what are you doing?!!"

"I'm gunna distract it!!"

---

*   which meant she was going in the opposite direction than everyone else, which made it a lot harder and a lot longer to get through.

Chapter Twenty

Bloat or Float

Evie hoped she was doing the right thing. The further away from the Bridge she ran, the more she thought it was a stupid, pointless idea. There'd be more movement in the Bridge. One girl running and waving her arms about might not make a difference. I mean, if you were an Ogrimite, feeling very hungry, and you felt a little bit of movement to your right and a lot of movement to your left, which direction would you go? Left or right?

Yep. Evie thought the same. Left. Of course left. More movement meant more food. But she had to try. Paulo and Squirt were sensible. They would get people on the Bridge to make the least amount of movement possible. Wouldn't they?

She was at a spot now that she thought was a good distance away from the Bridge. She felt absolutely silly, but she started jumping around and waving her arms about. She ran up and down the little length of corridor she was on, flapping her legs up as much as she could with each stride.

Mmmrrrreeeerrrrrgh! She could hear it somewhere near. Her heart was racing. It felt like the way hearts throb on cartoons—jumping right out of her chest and then back again, out, in, out, in. And the booming of its pump was throbbing in her head. Beating like a huge drum, its vibrations ricocheting through her whole body.

Is this even going to work? she questioned.

Mmmrrrreeeerrrrrgh!!!

Yes! It sounded nearer. Then all of a sudden, she had an enormous, terrifying revelation and she said out loud, "Argh! It's after me!"

She made sure she had a few clear escape routes, and continued jumping and twirling around, almost giving herself a headache. "This has got to be the craziest thing I've ever done," she thought out loud, then her voice quivered, "And I'm scared. I am *really* scared."

"This has got to be the stupidest thing she's ever done!" James said to Lisa soon after Evie had bolted. Immediately, James took off after her, but a hand had grabbed onto his arm, stopping him.

"You can't, James!" Lisa shouted over the noise.

"She's my sister! I have to!"

"What are you going to do? Run after her? You'll only attract its attention to you—probably both of you. You won't have achieved anything."

"But Evie's doing that *deliberately.*"

"I know. But I reckon she knows what she's doing."

James replied angrily, "So in other words, *Evie's doomed, why waste two lives.*"

"That's not what I meant at all! Evie's almost like a sister to me as well! Look we could be helping by getting as many people as possible to not move again."

"That would only draw more of the Ogrimite's attention towards my sister."

"But that's what's meant to happen."

"What?!"

"I mean it's what Evie set out to do! Come on, she'll be alright! Trust her instinct!"

James was in agony. He raked his fingers through his hair. "I could lose my sister!"

Lisa waited for him to make up his own mind.

Suddenly, they heard Paulo's voice. "Hey, you guys! Lisa and er . . . James! I could really use your help over here!"

"Sounds like we're needed here," said Lisa.

James took another glance out to the corridors. There were two different ways she could have gone. And lots of different ways within those two routes. He'd have a very small chance of finding her. He prayed quickly, then took a breath and closed the Bridge door and locked it.

He and Lisa ran to where Paulo was. The room was slowly becoming less and less crowded, but Paulo had run into a bit of trouble.

"The amount of use this mechanism's getting is starting to overload it!" he said urgently. "Lisa, I need you to hold this button down for me every time we're ready to send a group off for three seconds."

She nodded her understanding.

Paulo then took James over to where Squirt was by the transmat beams. "James, I need you to take over Squirt's job for me. Know what to do?"

James nodded and Squirt just gave him the essentials: to make sure the glass doors are properly closed before sending them off, to not put anymore than one person in each tube, and to work fast.

Paulo then brought Squirt back over to the teleportation control panel. "We need to connect the auxiliary power* onto the mechanism, and fast. I'm not sure how much longer the other's going to handle."

"But that could take away some of the power from the engines. We could fall out of orbit, ♦ or start breaking down."

"This satellite's going to be blown to smithereens soon anyway, we can take the chance."

"Rightio." Squirt got down onto the floor on his back and pulled himself underneath the control panel. While he opened secret compartments, entered codes and rearranged wires, Paulo handed him the tools.

After a short while, Paulo was happy again with the way the teleportation mechanism was working.

"Well that's done the trick I think," said Squirt standing up. "But the satellite's in a pretty unstable condition now. The auxiliary power's meant to be for the engines, not menial things like matter transfer.

"Well Squirt," Paulo said, patting a hand on his shoulder, "as long as the engines don't run out of power mysteriously, we'll be fine. Look, we've only got about twenty people left."

James suddenly called from his post. "Paulo? Are you able to see what's happening through the rest of the satellite from here?"

"Yes, I can get a visual display of just about every room and corridor, why?"

"Try and find Evie, will you?"

"Evie? What's she . . ."

"Just find her!"

---

* which of course means the reserve or back-up power.

♦ Bad news of course if you're relying on the orbit of the satellite around Serothia to stay alive.

Paulo turned on a monitor which was not far from the teleportation control panel. He pressed buttons to flick through the numerous different camera surveillance views throughout the satellite. After flicking a while, they saw Evie. James was relieved to see her and without taking an eye off the screen, he carried on with his job quickly and efficiently.

There she was. Jumping, running around in circles, doing a monkey impression, skipping back and forth and shouting something. There was no audio on the monitor, but by the way her lips were moving it looked like *come on you big blob of blue blubby . . . blegh! Oi! Ogrimite, over here! . . .* that sort of thing.

Although something like this would usually make James laugh, he couldn't. This seemed like a suicide act. He continued to pray under his breath, and from now on, he didn't stop.

"Someone keep an eye on that screen. When she's at the Bridge door, we open it straight away," James said.

As Paulo watched the screen, he frowned. What a wonderful thing she was doing, he thought, but he felt sad for her and her brother. He knew how fast an Ogrimite could move when it wanted to. He'd seen everyone of his crew mates dead because of it. As far as he was concerned, Evie didn't have a hope

"Poor Evelyn," he said under his breath. "Poor James."

BANG!!!

There was an enormous jolt and everyone was shaken to the ground.

Alarm loudly beeping.

"What was that?" asked Lisa wide-eyed and terrified.

Squirt slowly got onto his feet and looked around, also wide-eyed. "It sounded like . . ."

Paulo raced to the main control deck and frantically observed the readings. "It's one of the engines," he said with dread. "One of the engines has packed up!"

"What's the course?" Squirt asked confused.

"Unknown. But I bet I can guess." Paulo then raced to the surveillance monitor.

There was another crunching sound and a terrible jerk. All on board were again thrown onto the floor. Up on the monitor, they could see that Evie also got flung into a wall and then tumbled into a heap on the floor.

Evelyn picking herself back up was the last James saw of her, as Paulo flicked through all the other possible areas of the satellite, taking Evie off the screen. Lots of different rooms and corridors came up—all wide open empty spaces or passageways. Until suddenly, Paulo saw a flicker of blue. He pressed buttons to go back to the right camera view. And as he had suspected, the Ogimite was in full view in the power core room of the satellite. Paulo imagined that it was looking up at the camera sniggering, as if it knew Paulo was watching it.

"What is it?" Squirt asked, stumbling up behind Paulo.

"The Ogrimite sabotaged one of the engines."

There was another horrible grating sound and the men were lurched to one side.

"And he's about to destroy another one," said Paulo.

"How many engines are there?" Lisa asked.

"Three."

"I'd better try and keep control of this thing!" Squirt said, running to the main controls and sitting down at the operator's chair.

"What happens if it destroys all the engines?" Lisa asked.

"We'll probably lose orbit and from there we'll just float in space without stopping. Eventually running out of oxygen."

"Whoa," she said softly.

"I know, fascinating isn't it!"

"Hang on," shouted James from where he was, still getting people into the tubes, "the Captain's blowing this place up, we can still all escape!"

"If we lose orbit, we lose contact with Serothia, and therefore with the broadcasting centre. If there's no connection, he's got no way to blow us up."

BANG!!!

"There goes another engine!" announced Paulo.

The others were tossed to the floor and the alarm was ringing loudly in everyone's ears.

Squirt was heaving at levers and generally being thrown around in the chair.

It was very hard for the Earth people to walk straight to be able to get into a tube and James was having a lot of difficulty closing the glass rotating doors.

He'd just managed to close a door and Lisa pushed the button Paulo had instructed her to.

There were seven people left. Not including James and Lisa.

"Quick, you five, get in!" James said. "Time?!!" he called out.

Squirt could not stop what he was doing to look. "Forget it!!" he yelled back.

"Right, last two, in you get," James said.

Paulo came away from the monitor and took over from Lisa again. "This is it, you two. It's your turn, there's enough room."

"But Evie," James said. "Look it's worked out perfectly, there's one more spot for Evie, we'll wait."

"She'll come any minute," Paulo said. "You four need to go now, I'll send her through as soon as she comes."

"But, but . . ."

There was another violent jolt. James and Lisa were hanging onto the control deck.

"Come on, there's not a second to lose."

"Quickly! Hurry up!" the two people already in the tubes were calling.

Without saying another word, James was hustled into one of the tubes—Lisa in the one next to him.

"All the best!" Paulo said before he shut the glass door. "Thanks for all your help!!"

"No worries, but . . ."

"Evie will be right with you."

Lisa gave a wave and Paulo waved back as he pushed the button and held it for three seconds. They were gone. He didn't know why he had told James Evie would be right with him. He didn't believe what he had said. He wasn't sure whether he was just showing optimism or whether he'd plainly . . . lied, to save James' feelings.

Paulo quickly checked the monitor, flicked it back to where Evie had been seen. She was gone. Paulo's stomach sank. But wait . . . if she'd been killed, her body would still be there. He flicked through the different rooms and corridors again, saw the Ogrimite still trying to dismantle the last engine in the power core, but couldn't find Evie. He wished he knew what to do. Squirt made up his mind for him.

"Paulo, we can't spend any longer in here, we've got to go."

"We can't, what about Evelyn?"

"Would you prefer being blasted to smithereens, or left to decay in deep space? They're your only two options if we stay here any longer!" Squirt had stood up from the controls and started dragging Paulo to the Bridge doorway. He unlocked it and they both went bolting out, calling Evelyn's name.

On the way to the Train, they did not encounter Evelyn.

"How much time?" Paulo asked.

Squirt looked down at his timer, "Twelve seconds. We've got to be in that craft."

While Paulo was still calling out for Evie, Squirt felt around for the side of the Captain's space craft. When he found it, Paulo could stall no more. They had to get on. They climbed in with eight seconds on the timer. Squirt went straight to the engine room to make sure everything was functioning properly and getting ready for take off. If it wasn't, Squirt had no idea what to do about it, but luckily, the engine was beginning to roar and it was making its rhythmic chuffing sound, louder and louder, faster and faster. Paulo had just come up behind Squirt, intrigued at what he had already seen of the Captain's vessel.

Five, four, three . . .

"Quick, close the door!!" said Squirt.

And Paulo, feeling extremely guilty and devastated by the thought of Evelyn, dashed back to fasten the door closed, ready for the scheduled return flight to Serothia.

A millisecond after the Train had fully dematerialised, and just as the Ogrimite had destroyed the last engine, the satellite ignited. It was reduced down to nothing but space dust.

Chapter Twenty-One

Evelyn's Story

One perfectly average night, me, my brother James and my friend Lisa were driving along a dark road to Summer Camp. We got a flat tyre, I went to see what it was we ran over, and I met this man who wanted me to call him Captain. Then James and Lisa disappeared and the Captain said he could find them.

I begged him to let me come with him.

He took me to a planet called Serothia, millions of light years away where a satellite was in trouble because its crew were dead men. James and Lisa reappeared on this satellite, along with hundreds of other people from Earth. They were stuck there and more and more were coming and it couldn't be stopped. Plus, there was an unstoppable, devouring creature, which looked like a giant blue pulsating blob on the loose in the satellite, who wanted to take over Serothia. I thought that things could not get worse, but the Captain's manner was so casual and confident,

I trusted in him when he said he could fix it all.

He said he had to go down to the planet's surface—I had to stay behind and help on the satellite. But I wanted to see Serothia, so I snuck on board the Captain's Train when he wasn't looking and hid under the valance of one of the sofas.

I'm glad I did.

On Serothia I burst into people's homes, I almost got brainwashed by watching T.V., I got kidnapped by a strange man with a gun, locked in a dark room*, rescued by the Captain and someone called Squirt and then whisked back up to the satellite.

That was the last time I saw the Captain. Back on the satellite, we had just ten minutes to get all those hijacked people back to Earth, including me, my brother and Lisa, before the Captain blew up the satellite—all while a killer movement-sensitive alien stayed on the prowl. Unfortunately, many didn't make it back to Earth. I was one of them. You see, when I heard the Ogrimite coming, I knew that I had to draw it away from the crowd so that they had a chance to get home. I didn't think. I just ran. I ran far enough away from everyone else and started to move about like a lunatic. When I heard the Ogrimite coming closer to me, I knew my plan had worked. It was coming after me instead of all those poor people wanting to get home—including James and Lisa.

I saw it eventually. And it was coming towards me—fast. I froze. Not by choice, but by fear and I knew that not moving was how to stay alive anyway. I just stood there, staring at it, and soon, it walked away. And I learnt something valuable. An analogy for life, I guess you could call it. Sometimes, the only way to solve your problems in life, the only way to conquer your fears is if you face them. When you face your problems, they just flee. But if you flee instead, run away from them, they only get bigger and they can totally destroy you.

So the monster was leaving. Then I worried, because it would now be after all those people again. The people I

---

*   Literally, a *dark* room—where photographs are developed.

was trying to save. So I moved around like a lunatic again, but it didn't come. No matter how much I moved, it didn't come. Then came this horrible sound and I was thrown to the floor because of a violent jolt. This ear-piercing alarm came on and the banging and jolting kept on happening. I had no idea what was going on and I had no idea what to do. Time was ticking on. The satellite could have blown up at any moment. Decisions. Decisions. This was life and death! No exaggeration, it really was! I was convinced that there must have only been seconds left before the inevitable explosion, so I sprinted (faster than I'd ever sprinted on any school sports day) in the direction of the Bridge—my way home. But then I thought of something. People say that in the moments before death, an individual can think about the oddest little things. Pointless things. Things that don't matter in the grand scheme of life. Well I thought about my favourite jacket. I'd left it on the Train. When Squirt and I were on our way back to the satellite, I'd taken it off because it was hot in there. It's my favourite jacket. I had to go back. I know it sounds dumb. I got to the Train, quicker than what it would have taken me to get back to the Bridge, found it, in all its invisibleness, and rushed in with the intention of rushing straight back out, but I collided head-on with Paulo and we both fell on the floor of the Train . . .

"Before I knew what was happening, he was dragging me into the Train and he slammed the door shut behind me. I could hear the *chuffety chuff*ing of the engine getting louder and faster and then there was a bit of a loud screech and then everything was quiet," Evie was saying as her, Squirt, Paulo and the Captain were strolling up Jarzba street, Serothia. "I looked up ahead and there was Squirt at the controls of the Train. He was looking at me. And Paulo was looking at me. And then suddenly . . ."

"Squirt raced over to join me and we gave you a huge big hug!" Paulo said.

Evie laughed. "More like, smothered me, I couldn't breath!"

"Well I thought you were dead. Or *going* to be at any second."

"I was so glad to see you Evelyn," said Squirt. "I mean, I *was* the one who was hurrying Paulo up saying we had no time to look for you and that we had to get out of there quick or we'd either blow up or be destined to drift away and slowly lose oxygen. I mean, my words may have sounded quite selfish at the time, but we were all very desperate and words can't express how relieved I was to see you! Not just because I would have felt guilty if you didn't show up or anything like that, but becau . . ."

"It's alright, Squirt," Evie butted in, "I understand. Don't worry about it."

"You could write that whole adventure as a short story and sell it, Evie," said Paulo smiling.

"Well, that's how I'm going to write it in my journal. Except, by the end it sounds too . . . I don't know, not poetically flowing enough."

"I liked the bit about facing your problems," said the Captain after staying quiet this whole time. "That's profound. Now, you could write a book about that. Lots of people could relate to that."

"Well I think it's a lesson I needed to learn," she said a little shyly. Then she looked at each of them, looked them in the eye and they all stopped walking. "I . . . cheated in a test last year, at school. It was our last maths test, a really important one." She lowered her head now and swallowed. "My friend found out, and since then, she's been getting me to do her homework for her and if I don't, she'll tell Mr Brack what I did. She'll carry on again this year 'cause I didn't think I'd ever face up to it." She looked up again at them. "Well, as soon as I get back to school this year, I'm going to tell the teacher myself about the test. I don't care if I have to sit the test again or if I get a detention or something, I just want the whole thing to go away."

"I think you'll find it will as soon as you're honest," said the Captain.

Evie breathed in and out. She then gave a little smile. "I already feel like a little weight's lifted just telling you guys. And the thought of telling Mr Brack . . . well, it's scary but . . . well, Tanya won't be able to blackmail me anymore. I feel so relieved!"

"She doesn't sound like much of a friend to me," said Squirt.

Evie now had a big grin. "Thanks guys . . . I think this year's gunna be good."

Then the Captain changed the subject, and started to quicken his pace again. "Come on, we're almost there." He broke into a run and the others did the same.

They were heading towards the Satellite Training Base where both Paulo and Squirt had originally come from. At the gate, was Marak Neeper, like he often was.

"Stretch!" Squirt exclaimed as soon as he saw him, but he restrained himself from running over to him. He asked the Captain quietly, "Is he still, you know, being controlled by the Ogrimite?"

"Well the Ogrimite that was controlling him is, alas, no longer alive so he should be okay but . . . well . . . let's go and find out huh?"

The Captain and Squirt led the way over to the big gates, patrolled by the short, stout man.

"Stretch?" Squirt said warily.

The man wasn't facing them, so it was hard to tell whether he was back to normal or not. It was a little bit spooky, just seeing the back of his head. Squirt had an image in his mind of Stretch suddenly turning around, evil-eyed, pointing a gun at them.

He called his name again softly as they came up closer. And he suddenly turned around.

"Yeah?" His eyes were normal. Immediately, he recognised a face. "Squirt? Squirt! Wha'are you doing there? You should be in 'ere, training." His voice was normal. Good ole' Stretch's voice.

"I was out here, saving your life, as a matter of fact."

The Captain tapped Squirt's arm, gently reminding him not to be so sure straight away that Stretch was back to normal. He had fooled Evie first.

"Ey?" said Stretch.

"I don't suppose you remember anything that happened," Squirt said cautiously.

"When?"

"What's the last thing you remember, Marak?" asked the Captain.

"You, asking that question just then. Who are you anyway? How do you know my name?"

"What do you remember before this? About two minutes ago?"

"Two minutes ago?" he said, utterly confused. "I was just patrolling this gate. I admit I went inside for a coffee earlier but . . ."

"How earlier?"

"It was about three o'clock, only seven or eight minutes ago."

"It's half way to six now," said Squirt.

"Impossible." He looked at his watch. Squirt had been right. "That's strange. Although, I thought it'd gotten dark quick."

The Captain stepped forward. "He's free of the Ogrimite, but let me just double check . . ." He walked up close to Stretch and held up his index finger. He moved it to and fro in front of his face and asked him to follow it with his eyes. He then whipped out a small metal object and hovered it over Stretch's hair and observed a reading it gave. Then he took a pair of scissors out of one of his pockets, said "do you mind?" and clipped a small bit of Stretch's fingernail off and inserted it through a little slot in another gadget he'd pulled out of his pocket, flicked a switch and there was a faint crackling noise. Then he smiled. "I was right," he said, putting his tools away. "He's quite his old self again. Whatever that was."

"And what about everyone else?" Evie said.

"Well like I said, there's no longer a connection with the Ogrimite because the Ogrimite is no longer in existence. Now assuming everyone was brainwashed by the same Ogrimite . . ."

"Everyone will be free."

"And that Ogrimite was the only one ever on board the satellite making transmissions," Paulo said.

"That we *know* of," the Captain said raising his index finger. "Ogrimites are very good hiders, you know. They can mould themselves into any shape."

"Yes, I know," said Evie.

"What am I doing?" the Captain suddenly said, "I can't stand out here chatting all evening, I must go and see if our plan worked! Squirt er . . . will you try and explain to your friend as best you can? There's a good chap!" He turned in the direction of the training complex, but then stopped and added, "And persuade him to open the gate for me, will you?"

Evie and Paulo sidled through the gate after the Captain and followed him straight to the front desk.

There was a tall, stocky man with orange overalls behind it, sorting through some mail.

The Captain was in a hurry. "Quick, switch on the radio."

"Nothing but ads on."

"No, not that radio, the receiver, the receiver. Where is it?"

"Where is your authorisation?"

"I have it from Stretch out there."

"I need to see a pass, Mr. And for you two as well."

Paulo spoke, "Rayan, it's me, Paulo, remember? I got called up to work on the satellite a while back?"

"Oh yeah. Your face is familiar."

"Well here's my employee identification and these are friends of mine."

"They need their own passes."

Paulo rolled his eyes, ran behind the desk and activated the radio himself. He turned up the volume but nothing was coming through. "Do you think we'll hear from them, Captain?" he asked doubtfully.

"Allow me." The Captain reached across and Paulo gave him the microphone. "The two united Ogrimite tribes of Rasca, come in if you read me."

All of a sudden there was a surge of radio static and then some grim, groaning noises. They sounded similar to the groaning of the Ogrimite up on the satellite.

"Is that them?" asked Paulo.

"That's them," said the Captain.

Paulo feared the worst. The groans sounded like shrieks of anger and determination—even victory. *It's no good*, he thought, *they're still going to invade. There must be thousands of them up in the skies, ready to swoop down. Or perhaps they're going to wait until we build Satellite SB-18 and then try the same thing again and we'll never be free.*

All this time, the Ogrimites had been talking. The Captain acted as though he could understand what they were saying. Suddenly, he spoke back.

"The planet wasn't yours to take."

More groaning.

"Oh, don't give me so much credit, please! Anyway, I gave you a choice. And your leader or whoever he was refused to comply. He made the wrong choice. He brought this onto your entire race himself!"

More horrible noises.

"Well I'd advise you to go somewhere else and fast, but if you come anywhere near this planet again, you'll be sorry."

There was the fiercest roar from the receiver, and Paulo was still afraid of what they had said. He feared for the future of Serothia.

Chapter Twenty-Two

Table For Four

The Ogrimites were groaning something terrible. Paulo didn't like to imagine the kind of threats and hostile words they were saying. Even Evie had a sinking feeling. She felt that all of their troubles had been for nothing. Serothia had lost their satellite for nothing. People had died for nothing.

The Ogrimites were still raging, and the tone of it gave the others in the room a horrible chill. But suddenly, the Captain smiled and said casually, "Good." He switched off the radio communicator. "Right, that's that sorted out."

Paulo showed his puzzlement. "What did they say?"

"They said . . ." he put on a low grumbly voice, "We will leave and never return. Serothia be cursed."

"Really?"

"Yes," he said happily.

"They're going to put a curse on us?"

"Oh, you don't want to believe in that guff!"

"You mean, Serothia's safe?" Evie said excitedly. "The plan worked?"

"Yes."

Evie let out a huge yelp of joy, jumped over and hugged the Captain. Then she hugged Paulo as well. Paulo felt odd. It was not a popular custom on Serothia.

The Captain addressed the man who had been behind the desk and still hovering, "Thanks for that. Oh by the way, there's no longer a satellite up there. Small price to pay for the survival of a whole planet wouldn't you say?"

Paulo thought ahead of all the rebuilding and re-establishing of television, radio and iStream networks. The satellite played a major role in Serothians' lives. He wasn't looking forward to all of that. He'd be training in this place until another satellite was in operation again—being taught stuff he already knew. But he'd probably be given a senior role and some responsibility of training other people . . . *whoopty-do*, he thought, sarcastically.

The four were still together late that evening, walking along a road, still talking about their experiences. The Captain commended Squirt and Paulo for the job they did on the satellite. And lastly, he commended Evie, but his feelings towards her bravery were mixed.

He was about to reprimand her for taking so many risks and always tending not to do as she was told when he had to suddenly stop, "Oh, er . . . just a minute . . ."

He disappeared inside a building, and the others, puzzled, followed him in. They approached a tall desk inside the building. It looked very much like an upper-class restaurant.

The Captain spoke to the gentleman standing behind the desk rather stylishly. "My name's Captain Ringoes, I have a reservation, only . . . we have one extra, unexpected party, will that be a problem?"

"Not at all, Sir. It's very easily rectified. This way, please."

The gentleman in a very smart tuxedo glided through the restaurant, followed by the Captain, followed by three very baffled young people. Evie felt strange walking into a place like this, being treated like this, when she was wearing jeans and a hooded jacket, and she was with one man wearing orange long-sleeve overalls and another man wearing a light blue jumpsuit.

"Here we are Sir, the corner booth, as you requested. Here are the menus."

"Thank you *very* much."

"Take all the time you need." The man—obviously a waiter, turned to leave, but saw Evie, Paulo and Squirt still standing and said, "Please! Take a seat. Make yourselves comfortable."

They did as they were told, mouths open.

The Captain was sitting casually looking over the menu. "The lemon sorbet sounds delicious, though I suppose it's traditional to start with the savoury courses, er . . . how about the ostern steak smothered in seanut shell sauce? My my, try and say that ten times fast."

Evie just managed to speak. "How did you get us in here? No one ever in the world . . . in any worlds could be called Captain Ringoes."

"I had a reservation, obviously. You can't get into a good place like this of an evening without a reservation. Everyone knows that. What is ostern by the way?"

Paulo answered, "It's a field animal. When did you have time to make a reservation?"

"Anything like beef?"

"Beef?" asked Squirt.

"You know, cows. Mooooooo!"

"Oh, mooooooo! Yes, ostern sort of go moooooo. But more like maaaaarr."

"Oh, sheep."

"Sheep?"

"Never mind the ostern whatever it's called," said Evie. "As if you had time to stop and make a reservation!"

"Well aren't you just glad I did. Now we can enjoy a really top class meal. I hope. Ever been here before, you two?"

Paulo and Squirt shook their heads. The look on their faces told Evie that they probably would never be able to afford to come to a place like this.

"Anyway," said the Captain, "as I was about to say Evelyn, you're a naughty girl and I don't know whether to pat you on the back or whack you over the head for taking the risks you did."

"Yeah but my efforts didn't do all that much."

"Yes they did by the sounds of it. If you didn't distract the Ogrimite when you did, it might have got onto the Bridge before it decided to damage the engines."

"If it could get through the Bridge door. We still don't know if it could or not."

"I don't doubt that it would have. The way they can change their shape. Why, they could mould into the shape of a key if they press their bodies onto the lock hard enough. You saved the day."

"That reminds me of this woman. If it weren't for her, a lot more people might be dead. She helped me to get everyone to stop moving and that. I didn't even find out her name . . . She called me a hero. But that's because of this whistle of mine. I blew it, really weakly, and it scared the Ogrimite away."

The Captain frowned.

"Can I see it?"

"Yes!" she said eagerly, "I dropped it when I collapsed at the time, but I found it again on my way to distracting the Ogrimite." She took it out of her favourite jacket's pocket and put it on the table.

The Captain picked it up and examined it. It was a perfectly ordinary whistle.

"A blow from this wouldn't normally frighten something like an Ogrimite."

"Well when I was about to die in front of it, I felt this . . . I don't know, urge or something, to get it out and blow it. And whatever it was that I did, worked!"

The Captain's frown slowly turned into a subtle, knowing smile, as if he'd just remembered a personal joke and was inwardly laughing.

"That's another strange thing I can add to my 'strange things' list!" said Squirt, enthusiastically. "The other thing was, the time. Now I don't know about you two, but I felt the time went on and on and on. Are you sure that only was ten minutes you waited, Captain?"

"Of course. Ten minutes to the precise millisecond."

"Well that's not only my perception of the time, because, as a mere human, my perception of time could easily be warped and distorted. I mean for instance, when you're really busy or having fun, they say, time can go quickly and when you're bored, time can go slowly. Of course time isn't really going fast or slow, it's your perception, it *seems* like it's going fast or slow. So what I'm saying is that the time *seemed* to go slowly—from my perspective, but given the activity we were doing, being really busy and all, you'd think the time would seem to go fast—going by the unwritten theory I've just described. *So*, it can't have been just my perception of time going slowly because of this and also because of the fact that I calculated the time it would take to get nearly one thousand, five hundred people through the transmat beam and it was . . . well it was much longer than ten minutes." Squirt took a big breath.

The Captain stroked his chin. "I see what you mean."

"I felt the same," said Paulo.

Evie's mind suddenly went back to when she talked to God in the busy and stuffy corridor of the satellite. *God, couldn't you make time go really slow or something.* She'd prayed that prayer. And now here it was . . . they were talking about how unusually slow the time seemed to go.

"Have you decided yet?" asked the waiter, who had just approached.

"No, not yet," said the Captain.

"Perhaps you'd like to order drinks?"

"What a good idea. Evelyn?"

"Who's paying for this?"

The Captain pointed to himself.

"Alright then, I'll have a . . ." she didn't understand what any of the drinks were on the list. She went for the one that had an ingredient she recognised. "A lime and . . . duavafruit . . . frulè, please."

The rest ordered their drinks. Very exotic sounding, and Evie couldn't wait to see what would be placed in front of them.

"Well I think you deserve a clap too, Captain," said Evie. And Paulo and Squirt joined her in a little applause.

"No I hardly did anything. I did less than you, really. My life wasn't at stake. Not even my Train was at stake. If the whole thing went wrong, I would have been able to leave in my Train and carry on as normal. But I probably wouldn't have been able to leave come to think of it, when the planet would have still been at stake . . . Steak. I do feel like steak actually, I think I might go with the ostern steak smothered in seanut shell sauce. These seanut shells better be nice." He returned his attention to the menu. Then without looking up, he said softly, "Your brother and Lisa will be worried. They'll be glad to see you when you return."

Evie suddenly thought of them. They would have been expecting her back by the transmat beam. The longer she was here, the longer they would be worrying. In fact, the longer she was gone, the more they would be inclined to think that . . .

"They might think I'm dead!"

"Exactly. We'd better eat and run."

"Here are your drinks," the waiter came and said after a short while. They looked amazing.

"Just how are you going to pay for all this?" Evie said. "I didn't even think before, how have you gotten money on this planet? I don't get it." She could tell by the looks on Paulo and Squirt's faces that they didn't get it either. The look on the Captain's face, however, told her that he enjoyed having an air of mystery around him. He seemed like a straight forward guy, but he was so . . . not straight forward.

She was waiting for his answer, but the waiter interrupted. "Would you like more time to decide what to eat?"

"No, we'd better order now." He allowed everyone else to order before himself. Then, when the waiter had gone off with their orders, (the Captain having ordered the steak), raised his glass of red and yellow frothy drink and said, "Well, here's to Serothia. An uninvaded, brave, and beautiful planet."

"I'll drink to that!" said Squirt, and they clinked their glasses together, laughed, smiled and took a sip.

Evie's eyebrows rose at the powerful, but delicious taste.

"I think we ought to have a toast to the Captain as well," said Paulo. "Even though he won't accept the praise."

"Oh I'll accept it," he smiled. "But it wasn't just me."

"Well I thought it was all so impossible! Everything seemed impossible. If it was me by myself, I would have given up ages ago!"

"I told you we could do it, right from the start. I told you we'd get by with a little help from my friend."

Before Evelyn got a chance to feel pleased with herself, Paulo asked the Captain curiously, "Just who is this friend of yours, Captain?"

The Captain then spoke with the least enigmatic expression Evelyn had seen on him yet. He looked straight back into Paulo's eyes. "He's the Beginning and the End. The Ancient of Days, the Comforter and Commander. Creator of all things. The great I AM." Then he took another sip of his red and yellow frothy drink.

"Evie's not coming is she?" James said after many minutes of waiting—almost an hour. "Paulo said he'd send her straight away."

Lisa spoke with not much conviction, "Maybe there's some strange time variation when you go through one of those."

"Then why did all these people arrive in exactly the same place at the same time we did? It's worked for everyone else. All fifteen hundred or so of them. Except for Evie."

"I don't know. I don't know what to think. But we can't give up hope." Lisa eventually put a hand on James' arm. Then after a while she said, "Where are we, anyway? Where did we end up?"

"Don't know. It looks like somewhere in Europe. I think Paulo said it'd take us to where the last person came from. That was that tall man in the suit." He spoke in such a flat, sad tone.

"He had a sort of German sounding accent."

"Great, so we're in Germany."

"We'll find our way home."

"Well we're not going anywhere until we've got Evie with us."

"Of course not. We'll search and search until we've found her. There could be any explanation for why she's not here on this very spot."

"Yes. That's right," James said, lightening up.

"We'll be late for Summer Camp," Lisa tried to joke to lighten the mood. "Evie did stress she didn't want to get there and have to go to bed straight away."

It didn't make James smile much. He could not rest. And it was that way for a long time.

The Captain and Evie were saying farewell to Paulo and Squirt at the gate of the Satellite Training complex.

"I can't thank you enough for what you did," the Captain was saying and in turn, shook them both by the hand firmly.

"Well thank goodness you came along when you did," Paulo said. "I wouldn't have known what to do. I think we'd all have been doomed. And Squirt. Thank goodness you got a hold of Squirt," Paulo patted the tall young man on the back. "And to this friend of yours." Paulo's tone became more serious. "I'd like to learn more about this friend of yours. I mean, I didn't see anyone else. I mean . . . who is he, really?"

"He's er . . . hard to describe in a short sentence. In fact, he's hard to describe at all."

"Some people describe him as indescribable," Evie said. She was pretty sure she knew who the Captain was talking about. She thought she knew him as well. But this ordeal had made her rethink.

"Well, I'd better report back," said Squirt. "It was real exciting! A real adventure, really. And I'm honoured to have helped!"

"I think I'll miss you Squirt," said Evie. "It was real nice knowing you. And thanks heaps for rescuing me from that dark room."

Since Squirt didn't have a hat to tip, he rubbed the very tip of his black hair at the front of his head and tipped his head to her. He put on a hillbilly accent*, "It was my pleasure to rescue such a mighty fine purdy young lady like you."

Evie laughed and she gave him an impulsive hug.

---

*   Funny . . . they must have had hillbillies on Serothia—just like on Earth.

While this was happening, Paulo said quietly to the Captain, "I don't suppose . . . well I mean . . . your Train thing, I don't suppose there's room for a passenger . . . I mean . . . just for a short . . . well, what I'm trying to say is . . . I want to know more about this friend of yours and I was wondering . . . could I come with you. I mean, would I meet him if I came with you?"

"It's not my Train *thing*, it's called the *Train*. And are you sure of what you're asking?"

"I think so, yes. I mean, I've got nothing much to look forward to here. A position at the training grounds all builds up to having a job on the satellite. Well I've done that and well . . . it's not all that wonderful, really. I've done it all now. Everything I've been trained to do, I've done it."

"Why do you want to meet the Ancient of Days?"

Paulo thought about it for a moment. "Because he sounds wonderful."

"Bye Squirt!" Evie finished saying.

"Right, come on then," said the Captain starting to walk away.

Evie was surprised by his rushed farewell to Paulo. "Well, Paulo I'll miss you as well."

"No you won't," said the Captain.

"Don't be rude."

"I'm not. You won't miss Paulo. Not for another ten minutes or so yet. You can say your goodbyes then."

The two started walking off, Evie trying to keep up.

"What do you mean?"

"If you must know, Paulo is going to be my passenger for a while." The Captain put on his glasses.

"A passenger? Where are you going to?"

Paulo passed a glance at the Captain. "Nowhere in particular, I don't think."

"I want to be a passenger too, then."

"Impossible."

"Why not? I didn't know you took passengers before, but now I know, could I be one?"

"I don't take passengers . . ."

"Well you are though."

"What I mean is, I don't think of it as taking passengers. Anyway, you must get back to Lisa and Jamal so they know you're alive."

"What's so hard about *James?*" she suddenly stopped on the road and said with heat under her tone. "I mean, there's nothing strange or unusual about the name James. In fact, it's one of the most normal names in the history of names. It's even in the Bible. What is your problem with the name James?"

"Nothing. It's an excellent name. Closely related to the meaning: 'May God protect'. Extraordinary name. Ah, here we are."

The Captain reached into a pocket and pulled out a key.

"Here we are where?" asked Paulo.

"I think he means, here we are at the Train."

"How can he see it?"

"It's got something to do with his glasses I think."

He inserted a key into thin air and the next thing, a door swung open and they could see inside the cosy carriage.

All three stepped inside and the Captain led the way to the engine room. "Right Paulo, first I have to take this young lady home and then . . ."

"Can't I phone James and let him know I'm alright? He's got a mobile."

The Captain felt uncomfortable. Deep down, he felt that Evie would absolutely love a ride in the Train, but he also thought she was too young and was only concerned for her safety and wellbeing. He couldn't tell her that though, because he knew that she would think that was a lame excuse. It would also belittle her, and after risking her life to save others and putting herself in danger to have an adventure, he felt that was highly inappropriate.

He struggled to find the words. "You just . . . should be home with your family. It's ridiculous for you to choose me over them. You don't know me."

Neither does Paulo, were the words that came to her lips, but she swallowed them down. She knew he was right, and she was disappointed.

"I don't want to put you through that danger again. If anything happened to you, I would be responsible. Plus, I don't *want* anything to happen to you."

She nodded, looking at the floor. "I'm honoured to have helped," she mumbled, stealing Squirt's words. Then she said with more enthusiasm, "I loved seeing the stars! A whole new galaxy! You're amazing. I still don't know who you are and why you can travel around the universe in a tiny little modified train that makes a cup of tea!"

The Captain smiled warmly. "Come on. Let's get you home." He touched a lever and the engine's roar rose up loud as anything, and then the slow-to-begin-with **chuff** *choofety chuff, choofety* **chuff** *choofety bang!* began to sound and speed up and then there was the big thud. The Captain's face had changed. The thud, wasn't the usual thud. It was louder, heavier, and had a horrible screech to it. Plus, it was a very violent thud that had sent the three of them crashing to the floor, and there was a small explosion on the control panel. Sparks flying up.

The mechanical blinds on the windows had been shut, and the Captain was now trying to open them to get an image of what was happening outside.

"Meteor shower?" Paulo suggested while being tossed around on the hard floor.

"Collision with another satellite?" Evie wondered and hoped desperately that it wasn't.

"Can't be either of those things!" shouted the Captain. "The radar screen says there's nothing surrounding the outer hull of the Train!" He too was on the floor, but he had one hand on something sturdy to hold on to, and the other hand frantically fiddling with controls. "My controls aren't working! Nothing I'm doing is making the slightest difference!" As a test, the Captain hit the general alarm button. Not even this worked. "The controls are locked! I can't do anything! Quick, Evelyn, shovel some more coal in the furnace! You know where it is! You and Paulo, shovel as much as you can fit in! We need to try and get thrust from somewhere!"

Evie did so, headed straight for the Captain's special coal stash, opened the furnace door, grabbed a shovel and started shovelling. Paulo found a second shovel and did the same.

The Captain had now managed to stand up as well and he was trying to make sense of his controls. "This makes no sense," he said to himself. "These controls are never wrong!"

"What's it say?" Evie shouted.

"It says we're going back in time. And really, really fast! I can't stop it! 1991, 1973, 1805, 1633, 1211, 321 . . . you'd better get down on the floor, quick! I don't know when this thing's going to land, but it's certainly going to be a big crash!"

"But the furnace . . . !"

"Leave it now! You'll have to!!"

Evie and Paulo closed the furnace door, chucked the shovels away and took cover underneath one of the sofas in the carriage room.

The Captain was still trying to gain control of the Train, but it was no use! The Train was hurtling into the unknown and it was a mightily bumpy ride. "God protect us!!" the Captain said and took cover himself, for what might be the biggest and most devastating crash he had ever experienced. Not a physical crash, like the Train hitting the ground from a great height; but a time crash, which any time traveller knows, is much, much worse . . .

"Those whom I (God) love I rebuke and discipline. So be earnest, and repent."—Revelation 3:19

"Although he (Jesus) was a son, he learnt obedience from what he suffered."—Hebrews 5:8

"I can do everything through Christ Jesus who gives me strength."—Philippians 4:13

"There's nothing my God cannot do."—Job 42:2

"Moon Man" Facts

The Universe

There is a galaxy M64, which has a bright nucleus surrounded by a dark cloud of absorbing dust. This is what gave rise to its nick names of the "Black Eye" or "Evil Eye" galaxy. It is a spiral shaped galaxy and it is 17 million light years from Earth in the constellation Coma Berenices. There are more than thirty galaxies in this constellation.

The Captain's 'The Beatles' Quotes

"We'll get by with a little help from my friend"—from the actual song line "I get by with a little help from my friends" from the song "With A Little Help From My Friends"

"You say goodbye and I say hello"—from the song "Hello Goodbye"

"Let It Be" from the song "Let It Be"

Other

The name 'James' is a Biblical name derived from the Latin Iacomus or Jacomus, itself a derivative of Iacomus or Jacomus and thus sharing the same roots as 'Jacob'. 'Jacob' is from the Hebrew Yaakov or Yakubel, meaning 'May God protect'. [Pickering, D 1999, *Dictionary of first names: the essential guide for all parents*, 2nd Ed, Penguin Reference]